Night of the 'Double Moon

A Real Ghost Story

Viola arnald

Sarah Jane Singer

Published By
Computer Classics ®
497 Elysian Fields Road A-11
Nashville, Tennessee 37211

Night of the Double Moon © is published in e-book format by **Computer Classics** ® on the **Computer Classics** ® website www.computer-classics.com.

Editor: Edward Ronny Arnold
Cover Design: Edward Ronny Arnold

Computer Classics ® is a registered Federal Trademark

Library of Congress Control Number: 2004103790

ISBN: 0-9748870-9-9

Printed in the United States of America

Contents

Introduction

John Stepp wasn't worth a damn!

My mother and father didn't like him. My brother and two sisters didn't like him and I didn't like him. I once heard my father say, "John's mother and father don't like him." I never heard anyone saying anything good about John Stepp. So, I guess it was unanimous. Nobody liked John Stepp.

John was big and ugly. He looked like a bear. I don't think it was his size that people didn't like but his attitude. He was a bully. People were afraid of him. I know my father was afraid of him. When my father talked about John Stepp, I could tell it in his voice. My father was afraid of John Stepp.

John Stepp carried a gun with him at all times. It was not an ordinary gun but a special gun. The gun was a two-barrel shotgun that had the barrel sawed off. It was short and John Stepp carried in his arms. The gun didn't shoot regular shells. It shot dimes!

John Stepp took the shot out of the shells and he replaced it with dimes. He often made the claim, "When I go into a fight, I win!" John wasn't worth a damn! He never held a job except one. He was our constable.

My father said John Stepp became constable by one vote, his own. Two men were running for constable when John threw his hat into the race. The two men quit. They were afraid of John. When the

ballots were counted, John Stepp had one vote. No one voted for him. My father didn't vote for him. John was the only person who placed a mark by his name. He won by one vote. He would have won anyway because his was the only name on the ballot.

The young boys didn't like him. Abram didn't like him. Abram's real name was Abraham but everybody called him Abram. Abram had a run-in with John Stepp. He and two other boys were going to pull a prank on Miss. Agnes. Miss. Agnes was a widow. Her husband died a few years ago and she lived alone. She had a milk cow and Abram and two others were going to hide her cow in the woods. I don't know if they ever pulled the prank but John Stepp heard about it and he gathered the boys together. He took them to the jail and he locked them up.

Abram said John Stepp pointed that gun at them. He told them if they bothered Miss. Agnes or any other of the old folk, he would take them to the woods. Abram told my father that they believed John Stepp threatened to kill them. No one believed the story until one of the boys showed up dead.

People believed John Stepp killed the boy. Then, the second boy showed up dead. People began to talk. I remember hearing my father talk about the two boys and how he believed John Stepp killed them. Then, Abram died. The talk stopped because

John Stepp couldn't have killed him because he was looking for him. My father was with John Stepp when they found Abram. John tried to save him but it was too late.

I don't remember too much about John Stepp, as I was ill as a young girl. I don't remember much about him, except that night. I was very ill. I was nine years old. My fever was high and my mother placed cold, wet rags on my body. I would wake up and see John Stepp sitting by the door. He was holding that gun in his hands.

I remember being afraid. I saw John Stepp and I knew no one liked him. I knew he had that gun that shot dimes. He would smile at me but I was afraid of him. I would fall back to sleep.

The sound of John Stepp firing that gun woke me. I remember the load sounds and I remember that horrible scream. I also remember the sound of Andy's crow. When I heard Andy's crow, the first light came through my window. Somehow, I felt safe. I wasn't afraid anymore.

I don't remember much about John Stepp. What I remember of him was from that night. They were all there that night. My mother and father were there. My brother and my two sisters were there. John Stepp was there.

She was there!

She wasn't in our house she was standing by the woods. She stood by the woods near our gate. She came at sunset and she stood waiting. My father said she was waiting for me to die. He said she was waiting to take my spirit. John Stepp wouldn't let her take me. He wouldn't let her come near me. John Stepp fought her. He fought her with his gun that shot dimes.

They were there. They were all there, the night of the double moon.

Past Discretions

John Stepp drove the old truck along the wooded path. Oliver Brown sat beside him. They didn't speak as John drove. They had driven far, all the way from St. Louis. The truck was loaded with whiskey and it was the last run of the month. They had made three trips this month. Each truck was loaded with whiskey.

John turned the truck onto a small road. The road led to a clearing where they would unload the whiskey then; it would be taken elsewhere. As they approached the clearing, Brandon Caides was waiting. John began to slow the truck.

John turned to Oliver. "Something is wrong!" John said.

"What?" Oliver asked.

"Brandon is not waving! Something is wrong!" John said.

John slowed the truck. He stopped near Brandon. Brandon just stood still. He appeared to be motioning with his head. He was attempting to motion to his right. John reached into his coat pocket and he removed his gun. His gun was a sawed-off shotgun. The handle was trimmed down to the size of a pistol butt. Oliver reached into his coat and removed his pistol.

John slowly exited the truck. He looked to Brandon's right.

"Come out Knuckles!" John yelled.

Brandon just stood. There was a frightened look on his face. Oliver exited the truck and he came to stand beside John.

"Come out Knuckles!" John yelled.

"Knuckles isn't here!" a voice yelled from the woods. "He sent me!"

Several men exited from behind several trees. One man was tall and well dressed. The other men were burley looking. The burley men held axes in their hands. There were six men.

"Knuckles sent a professional to do this job!" the well-dressed man said.

John and Oliver looked at the men who held axes. They knew several of them. "Who are you?" John Stepp asked the well-dressed man.

"My name is David Logan. I am from St. Louis. Thanks for bringing the truck!" the well-dressed man said.

John stood with his gun held to his hips. "Brandon don't know nothing! Let him go! This is between the two of us!" John yelled.

David walked slowly toward John and he stopped. He looked at John's gun. "That sawed-off gun won't help you!" David yelled. "You're out of range!"

"Let Brandon go!" John yelled.

"Sorry!" David yelled.

John moved toward Brandon and he stood in front of him. He looked at the six men and he pulled the two hammers on his gun. "What ever Knuckles is paying you ain't worth your life!" John yelled. "What ever he's paying you ain't worth getting killed over!"

One of the burley men yelled, "We're going to chop you up into pieces and feed you to the hogs!"

Another burley man yelled, "We're not going to kill you! We're going to chop you up!"

"I get ten dollars!" he added.

David laughed, "I'm the one that's going to kill you! I get one hundred dollars!"

"It's not too late to turn and leave!" John yelled. "No man's life is worth ten dollars."

David laughed. He reached into his coat pocket and he removed a Colt pistol. The barrel was long, seven inches. He turned to the five men and he laughed. David raised his pistol. When he turned to look at John, Oliver, and Brandon, John fired his gun.

Kaboom! Kaboom!

John's gun jerked in his hands.

Smoke came from John's gun as a whistling sound was heard. Something smashed into David and two of the men. David's chest seemed to explode. David's eyes were wide open as something tore into his chest. David's right arm, that held the pistol, seemed to disappear.

The two men standing beside David flew backward. Oliver watched in horror, as the two men just seemed to fly backward. Before they flew backward, their heads seemed to disappear.

Kaboom! Kaboom! John fired his gun again. He had reloaded and walked forward. The gun was aimed at two men standing near to David. They held their axes upward as Oliver heard a whistling sound. Oliver saw the axes in the men's hands disappear. Their arms just seemed to vanish.

One man was left standing. He ran toward Oliver with his axe held upward. Oliver fired his pistol. The man stopped briefly as a bullet struck his shoulder.

Kaboom! Kaboom! John fired his gun again. The man with the axe flew backward. As he flew backward, his body separated. The top half went backward. The bottom half fell to the ground.

The smoke from John's gun was thick. Oliver and Brandon stood looking at John.

"What the hell did you have in that gun?" Oliver yelled.

John ejected two spent shells and he reloaded his gun. "Dimes!" John replied.

"Dimes! Dimes!" Oliver yelled. "You blew those men apart!"

"It was self-defense!" John said. "It was us or them!"

Oliver walked backward. "No!" Oliver said. He waved his hands into the air. "Those men didn't have a chance!"

"Neither would we!" John said. "They would have killed all three of us! I know of David! He was sent to kill us not to frighten us."

Oliver walked backward. "No! No!" Oliver yelled as he dropped his pistol. "Not this! I don't want no part of this!"

Oliver and Brandon ran from the truck. They ran toward the woods.

John Stepp stood looking at the remains of the six men. He walked carefully towards them and he held his gun ready. They were dead! They were all dead!

John returned to the truck and he unloaded the whiskey. When he had finished, he placed the remains of the six men in the back. He picked up Oliver's pistol and he placed it in his right coat pocket. Then, he drove the truck to the sheriff's office in Lebanon.

Oliver's Search for Redemption

Several days passed and Oliver Brown stood outside a small building in St. Louis. The building was very old and it connected to a Catholic Church. The building was a seminary for Catholic priests. Oliver stood for a long while before he walked to the door. He approached boldly and he knocked.

Several priests had been watching Oliver stand near the door. They watched from a side window. When Oliver knocked, the priests moved backward. They would not open the door. An older priest stood with them. He had been watching Oliver. The older priest walked to the door and he opened it.

Oliver stood at the door. Slowly, the door opened. "What do you want?" the older priest asked.

The older priest looked at Oliver. Oliver was very dirty and he looked hungry. It was late, almost eleven o'clock at night. Oliver looked at the priest and he lowered his head.

"What do you want?" the older priest asked again.

Oliver raised his head. "I want to become a priest!" Oliver answered. "I want to serve the Lord!"

The older priest smiled. "Come in!" he said. He opened the door and Oliver walked inside.

The Election Speeches

The town of Gladeville was full of excitement. The elections were not far away and men were campaigning. There was a platform near the post office and men were giving speeches. Ray Burgess and Harold Sanderson were on the platform. They were running for constable.

Jason Goodman was laughing. He had introduced Ray and Harold. "You will have a tough choice!" Jason yelled. "Either of these two men will make a great constable!"

Ray and Harold stood. They waved their hands to the crowd and the crowd cheered. Then, everyone got quiet. Someone was walking toward the platform. Jason stopped laughing as he watched the man walk toward the platform.

The man was John Stepp!

John walked to the platform and he stepped onto it.

"This platform is for candidates running for constable," Jason said.

"I know," John replied.

John Stepp looked at the crowd. "I'm running for constable and I have a few words to say," John said.

The crowd began to whisper. "John Stepp!" they said.

Jason was unnerved. "Why John?" he asked. "This is a surprise!"

John looked at the crowd. "You all know me and you all know about my past," John said.

John looked at Ray and Harold. "I know Ray and Harold and they are good men. They are real good men. Jason is correct! Either man would make a good constable."

John lowered his head slightly and he looked up. "Sometimes a good man is not enough! Sometimes a man who is not so good is needed!"

"Oliver and I did some bad things in our past. I have done some things I am not proud of! I never." John paused. "We never did anything to hurt honest, decent folks."

John paused. "I never did anything to harm anyone decent!" he said. "I never did anything to harm women or children. We only sold whiskey to those that could afford it and to those who wanted it! If a man wanted whisky and he had children, we wouldn't sell it to him. Oliver and I didn't want any children going hungry."

"Bad things are going to happen to Gladeville and you need someone who can take care of those bad things. Ray and Harold are good men. Being a good man won't be enough!"

John paused and he glared at the people. "To stop it!" he said.

John paused. He looked at the crowd. The people were silent. They stood looking at John Stepp. "I can only promise that I will do everything in my power to keep Gladeville an honest, decent town," John said.

"If you're guilty, I'll get you! If you're innocent, I'll protect you!"

The crowd was silent. Ray and Harold began to whisper to each other.

"Thank you!" John said. He stepped off the platform and he walked away.

Constable John Stepp

It was almost one o'clock in the morning when the truck drove down the old road. Four men were inside. The truck was loaded with whiskey from St. Louis.

The night was dark and the headlamps of the truck shone a far distance. As the truck drove along, the driver saw something in the road. In the middle of the road, a man stood.

The driver began to slow. He stopped a far distance from the man. The man wore a long dark coat and a dark hat. The driver could see the man's hands. In his hands he held a short gun.

The driver stepped out of the truck. When the driver got out of the truck, the three others followed. The four men held pistols.

"Get out of our way!" the driver, yelled.

"You're under arrest for transporting whisky!" John Stepp yelled. "Drop your guns and you won't get hurt!"

One of the men yelled, "John Stepp! Is that you?"

"Hello Knuckles!" John replied. "David didn't earn his hundred dollars! The others didn't earn their ten dollars!"

The four men held their pistols upwards. They aimed their pistols at John Stepp.

John quickly crouched to the dirt road.

Kaboom! Kaboom!

Several weeks passed and two trucks drove along an old dirt road. It was very early in the morning. There was no moon and the woods were black. Each truck had one man in the cab. As the two men drove the trucks, twelve men sat in the back of one of the trucks. The driver of the first truck saw two barriers in the road. There were two lanterns hanging from the barriers and they blocked the road.

The two trucks stopped and the twelve men quickly emerged. Each man held a pistol. The two drivers emerged and the fourteen men walked to the barriers. They held their pistols and they looked around. They did not see or hear anything. Two of the fourteen men began to move the barriers.

A voice called from the darkness; "You are under arrest for transporting whiskey! Drop your guns and you will not get hurt!"

The fourteen men began to fire their pistols into the darkness.

Kaboom! Kaboom!

Kaboom! Kaboom!

Several weeks passed and Mr. Sanderson was driving along an old road. It was late! He approached two barriers setup to block the road. There were two lanterns hanging from the barriers. Mr. Sanderson stopped his truck and he walked to the two barriers.

"Is everything OK?" a voice called from the darkness.

Mr. Sanderson was startled. He looked to see John Stepp walk from the darkness. John was holding his gun in his hands.

"John Stepp?" Mr. Sanderson asked.

John Stepp walked toward the two barriers and he began to move them.

"It's very late! Is something wrong?" John Stepp asked.

"No!" Mr. Sanderson replied. "There is a problem with the machinery at the mill and I am going there to see about it."

John moved the barriers to allow Mr. Sanderson's truck to pass.

"Is this where it happened?" Mr. Sanderson asked. "I heard some men were killed near here! I heard the men were going to cause trouble in town!"

John Stepp looked at Mr. Sanderson. "Sorry about the inconvenience!" he said.

Mr. Sanderson went to his truck and he drove past the barriers. As he drove past the barriers, John Stepp replaced them.

Randall Lewis is Missing

I was ill a lot as a young girl. It was pneumonia. Before I was grown, I had it nine times. I would get ill, then I would get better. Several times I almost died. Somehow, I managed to pull through.

The year was 1928. I was nine years old and ill. I was too ill to go to school. We lived in a four-room house between Gladeville and Smyrna. We lived not too far from Fellowship Road and the church. The church was named Little Seed Tick. A bus would take us to school. I missed a lot of school that year. It was hard for me to make up what I missed. I stayed home until I was better. When we went to church, we would walk through the woods to Fellowship Road. The woods were near our house. There was a small road that passed in front of our house but we just walked through the woods.

Near the road was a gate. It was just a wooden gate. There was a rope that tied the door. The fence was made of logs that had been split and stuck together. If you stood at the gate, you could see the woods. They weren't far from the gate.

Our house had a small front porch that was covered. In the summer, we would sit on the front porch and listen to the rainfall. It made a nice sound on the tin roof. There was a window on the front porch and it was the window of my bedroom. When the sun rose, the light came through my window.

I was always sick and I had the big bed. I slept alone. I was the oldest of three. My younger brother was J.B. His name was John Brown but everybody called him J.B. He was eight years old. I had two younger sisters, Lizzie and Cleo. Lizzie was seven and Cleo was six. There was about one year between us. J.B., Lizzie, and Cleo slept in my bedroom. They had a small bed on the floor. My mother and father slept in the other bedroom. We had a kitchen and a front room.

We hadn't lived in the house too long. It seemed we moved a lot. We lived several places. The one place I really liked was Smyrna. I think I liked Smyrna because I wasn't sick much and I went to school everyday. This house was nice. My father was a sharecropper. He grew cotton, corn, and wheat. We had some hogs and chickens. We also had some cows. We had a horse that my father would ride. He would hitch it to a small wagon. We didn't have a car. Cars were real expensive and we didn't have much money.

My mother and father were good to us. We never had any big fights or anything like that. My mother and father always hugged us and told us they loved us. I never heard my mother and father argue much. When they did argue, it was about the same thing - John Stepp. My mother didn't like him and my father was afraid of him.

I think my mother didn't like John Stepp because of a story he told about her. I don't know if the story was true but my father would laugh when it was mentioned. The story was my mother was a full-blooded Indian. John Stepp had said that he met a man who knew my mother when she was young. The man said her name was Running Dove. She lived in the Smoky Mountains when my father met her.

I didn't know if my mother was a full-blooded Indian. I didn't know what an Indian looked like. I never saw one. My mother had dark skin and black hair. She had high cheeks but I never heard her speak Indian. If she did, I never knew it. I didn't know what words an Indian would speak.

The story gets longer as the man said my father bought her. My father bought her for a bag of coffee beans and a bag of dried beans. My father would laugh about the story and he would make jokes about coffee beans and dried beans. One of our neighbors, Joshua, said the story sounded like a dowry. If a man loved a woman, he would give a present to her father. It was called a dowry.

I don't think the story was true. My mother and father were married in Smyrna. I saw their wedding license. She was nineteen when she married. My father was twenty-four. We had a picture of my mother and father hanging on the wall. He was real tall and she was real small. My mother was very pretty.

I don't think it was the Indian story that bothered my mother but the last part. John Stepp said the man that knew my mother said her father sold her because she was touched. Running Dove was very pretty but no one wanted to marry her because she was touched. My father met her and he liked her. Running Dove was sold to my father, as a wife, for a bag of coffee beans and a bag of dried beans.

This part really made my mother angry. I wasn't sure what touched was but it must not have been good. My mother would get real upset sometimes and do strange things. Sometimes my mother would say strange things. My father said she was touched. What ever it was, my mother had it. Whenever anyone mentioned John Stepp, my mother would become touched.

John Stepp was our constable. Nobody liked John Stepp. I never heard anybody say anything good about him. My mother didn't like him. She would say, "John Stepp ain't worth a damn! He never did anything for anybody!" I guess after a time, I began to believe it. I didn't like John Stepp either.

John Stepp was big and ugly. His face had scars all over it. He had real bad skin when he was young and it marked his face. He didn't have any hair on his face because of the scars. His ears were big and his nose was big. John's eyes were dark. His eyes weren't blue or green they looked black.

My father said he was a bully. He was always picking on the smaller boys. John was the biggest boy in the school. When a fight started, John Stepp finished it. Nobody liked John Stepp. Everybody was afraid of him.

He always wore a black hat and he wore a long black coat. John was tall. He was about as tall as my father was but John was big. He wasn't fat. He was big. John Stepp looked like a bear in that black hat and coat. When I would see him, I would get scared. I was afraid of him and I didn't like him.

John Stepp carried a gun with him at all times. He had a long pocket inside his coat and he kept his gun in the pocket. The gun was a two-barrel shotgun. John sawed most of the barrel off and he carried it inside his coat. His gun didn't shoot shot it shot dimes.

John replaced the shot with dimes. My father said he opened the shells and poured the buckshot out. He packed the shell with dimes. When he shot the gun, the dimes would blow something all to pieces. I never saw or heard John shoot his gun except that night. He must have shot it ten to twelve times. Whatever he hit, he killed.

My father had a job at the mill. It wasn't a full-time job, just a few days. I was ill and I didn't go to school. I awoke late and I was sitting near the door when I heard the car. It was John Stepp's car. I knew it was John's car because of the noise. The fender made a rattling noise. John's car was a 1926 Ford Model T Tudor. It was almost new when he bought it. John bought it in Alexandria. He bought it from a man that was driving it when the tornado struck.

We had a tornado in June of 1928. It struck near the border of Wilson County and DeKalb County. I remember the month because John Stepp came to our house. He came asking for food or clothes to help the people.

My mother must have been touched that day because John Stepp was real polite. He told her that there had been a tornado and several homes were destroyed. He asked if we had anything to give. My mother gave him some eggs and a jar of fruit. I was feeling well and I watched John drive off. John had visited most of the families and asked for something. He drove a truck he borrowed from the sawmill and it was full of things. He drove the truck to Alexandria.

When my father came home, my mother said John Stepp pushed his way into our house. She said he flashed his badge and demanded she give him food. My father was real upset. He asked me what happened. "I don't remember," I said.

The story must have been true because a lot of people said the same thing. They said John Stepp flashed his badge and took food. When he brought the car back, people said he sold the food to buy the car. The car was all messed up from the tornado. A man was driving it when the tornado struck. The tornado knocked the car off the road. The front window was smashed and a tree had fallen on the roof. The sides were all beat up where things had struck it and the tires were flat. No one believed John could fix it but he did. John fixed it up. He fixed everything but that one fender. The fender made a rattling noise when he drove the car.

People were upset about John Stepp flashing his badge and demanding food. He was our constable and people were afraid of him. When he ran for constable, nobody voted for him. My father said John Stepp won the election by one vote, his own. When the ballots were counted, John Stepp had one vote. He was the only one who placed a mark by his name. He won because his name was the only one on the ballot. Ray Burgess and Harold Sanderson's names were on the ballot but they withdrew. They said they were afraid John Stepp would hurt them if they won.

I heard John Stepp's car and I looked out the window. My mother went to the door. She looked out and saw John getting out of his car. "What does he want?" she said.

John came to the door and he knocked. My mother stood by the door and she wouldn't answer. John kept knocking. Then, my mother opened the

door. She had a big smile on her face. "Hello, John!"
she said.

"Is Jay here?" John asked.

"No. He is working," my mother replied.

"I need to see him. I need his help," John said.

"Is something wrong?" my mother asked.

"Yes mam! Randall Lewis is missing! I need
some men to help me search for him," he replied.

"Jay is real busy. I don't think he will have the
time. The boy is probably somewhere drunk," she
said.

"I don't think so. He has been missing for two
days. I need some men to help me search the woods.
Will you ask Jay to contact me?" he asked.

My mother nodded her head.

"Is Sarah Jane OK?" John asked.

"She is better," my mother replied.

"Is there anything I can do to help?" John asked.

"No. We will get by," my mother replied.

"Thank you," John said. He turned and walked
to his car. My mother watched him get into the car

and drive off. She closed the door and she turned to me. "That man ain't worth a damn!" she said.

My father returned from work late. He was paid a little money and a bag of flour and a bag of corn meal. We ate beans and fried corn cakes for supper. I didn't feel well but I ate some. My mother and father argued about John Stepp. My mother said he was mean to her and he treated her with disrespect. My father didn't say anything about that. He said John had visited most of the men asking for help to search for Randall. None of the men volunteered.

My mother didn't want my father to volunteer. She didn't want him to go near John Stepp.

John was in and out of his office that day. He would check a section of woods and return. He waited most of the day for the men to come to his office. It wasn't really an office but a small building near the post office. It was made of wood with one jail cell. The jail cell was made of iron bars. There was a room with a desk and John slept in the back room. The back room had a small bed and a small stove. The stove was mainly used for heat in the winter and John kept a pot of coffee on top. He ate most of his meals at the diner.

John had searched most of the woods. He returned to his office to wait for help but no one showed. He looked at the clock. It was almost five o'clock. John moved the coffeepot from the stove and he made sure the fire was almost out. He locked the door and walked to the diner.

When John entered the diner, Miss. Louise brought him his usual, a ham sandwich and a cup of coffee. John had a map with him and he laid it out on the table. He had checked everywhere except the woods near the Hibdon Cemetery. The Hibdon Cemetery was the oldest cemetery in the area. It was called the Hibdon Cemetery because there were many members of the Hibdon family buried there.

The cemetery was used a lot before and after the Civil War. It wasn't used much now unless the person that died was poor. No one really owned the cemetery. There was no fee to bury a person. People who were poor buried their kin there. Many old tombstones were there. Some were as tall as John Stepp was. There was a large section of woods that went from the cemetery to Fellowship Road. There was about five square miles of woods.

John ate his sandwich and he drank the coffee. He paid his bill and left. When he left, Miss. Louise made a comment, "I hope he chokes on that sandwich!" Nobody liked John Stepp not even Miss. Louise.

It was almost dark when John drove his car to the Hibdon Cemetery. He parked near the front gate and he took a lantern from the trunk. John kept the car lights on to look at the map. He turned the engine off and he started walking toward an old road near the edge of the cemetery. The road hadn't been used in many years. At one time, it was a county road but it wasn't used anymore. The summer was still here and the trees were full of leaves. The woods weren't too thick. John was able to move easily around the trees.

John walked a far piece. He stopped and looked at the map. He turned and went another direction. He didn't know what he was looking for. John kept looking at the ground. He expected to see Randall lying somewhere on the ground. It never occurred to him to look up.

He stopped to pee. He checked the map again and he went another direction. He walked toward the oldest part of the cemetery. John walked a short piece and he stopped. He smelled something. It was pee! He turned and looked where he had came. He had walked about thirty yards. John had peed at a tree about thirty yards away. He stopped and took a deep breath. He smelled pee and he smelled mess.

John began to walk quickly in a small circle. He could smell the pee and mess. The smell got stronger then it got weaker. At several points, he couldn't smell it at all. He retraced his steps and he came back to where he first smelled it. He placed the lantern on the ground and he began to walk around the trees smelling. The smell was strongest where the lantern was setting.

He began to walk in a small circle again. The smell was strong, then weak. He walked about ten feet from the lantern when he saw something on a tree. He ran quickly to get the lantern and he shined it on the tree. There was a rope tied to the tree. John walked to the tree. The rope was new, that is why he saw it. It was brand new. It was one-half inch in diameter and tied in a strong knot.

The rope was stretched tight. It went upward into the trees. John couldn't see how far it went up. He shined the lantern upward and he tried to follow it. As he followed it, he walked backward to where the lantern had been sitting. When he walked back to where the lantern had been sitting, he looked upward.

He saw Randall's feet.

Randell's feet were about ten feet off the ground. John could only see his feet because it was dark and there were many leaves. He walked back to where the rope was tied. He counted his steps to where the lantern had set on the ground. John took a pencil and he wrote on the map. He drew a triangle on the map. John tried to calculate how long the rope was and how high Randall was. When he had completed his calculations, he lowered Randall's body.

Randall's body was stiff. He had been dead perhaps a day or two. His hands weren't tied. John looked at Randall's pants. There were stains where Randall had peed and messed on himself. He looked at Randall's feet. His feet weren't tied. John left the rope on his neck. He rolled the rope into a coil and placed it on Randall's chest. He carefully picked him up and carried him to his car.

It was late when John arrived at Dr. Sanders' home. He knocked on the door. Dr. Sanders was asleep. It took a while before he came to the door. When Dr. Sanders came to the door, John told him he had found Randall. The autopsy was quick. Dr. Sanders could find no sign of a struggle. There was no evidence that Randall's hands had been tied or that his feet had been tied. There were no bruises on his face. No one had struck him. When he removed the rope from Randall's neck, there were no rope burns around the neck.

Randall's shirt had blood on it where his nose had bled. His pants were soiled. Dr. Sanders could not find any evidence of a struggle. There were no bruises or any evidence that Randall had struggled. It looked like someone just hung him. Since there was no evidence of a struggle, it was suicide. Randall climbed a tree and hung himself.

John Stepp drove to Randall's home. Randall's parents were not asleep. They were sitting on the front porch. When Randall's mother heard the sound of the fender, she knew it was John Stepp. She knew he had found Randall and she began to cry. Randall's father met him by the road.

"Where did you find him?" Mr. Lewis asked.

John turned the car engine off and he exited his car. He could hear Randall's mother crying.

"I'm sorry," John said.

Mr. Lewis was angry. "Where did you find him?" he asked.

"It was near the Hibdon Cemetery. I found him in the woods. He hung himself," John replied.

"Where is he?" Mr. Lewis asked.

"He is at Dr. Sanders' home. If you like, I'll take you there," John replied.

Mr. Lewis hung his head downward. "Not now," he said. "Will you ask Dr. Sanders to prepare him?" he asked.

"Yes sir," John replied. "Will you bury him in the Hibdon Cemetery?" he asked.

"I guess so. We don't have any money," Mr. Lewis began to cry.

"I'll take care of everything. If there is anything I can do, let me know," John said.

Mr. Lewis didn't answer. He turned and walked to their porch. Mrs. Lewis was crying.

John Stepp cranked his car and then he got in. He sat for a few minutes looking at the Lewis house. Something didn't make sense. Randall was a good boy. He pulled pranks but he was a good boy. He never did anything real bad and he never got into any real trouble. Something was wrong. Randall couldn't have hung himself. Somebody murdered him.

John drove to Dr. Sanders' house and he told the doctor to prepare Randall. Then John drove back to the woods where he found Randall.

It was late in the evening when Joshua came to the house. He said John Stepp found Randall. He found him hanging from a tree in the woods near the Hibdon Cemetery. John was alone when he found him. He went searching, alone, after dark. Josuah didn't know much about the event. He heard Randall had hung himself.

The funeral was held the next day. I didn't go because I felt ill. My mother and my two sisters stayed with me. My father and my brother J.B. went. Mr. Lewis was real upset about his son's death. He and his wife Georgia only had one child, Randall. The service was real nice. Randall was at the Little Seed Tick Church. Reverend King said real nice things about Randall. His casket was a simple pine box. It wasn't opened. Randall didn't look real good and Mrs. Lewis didn't want people looking at his neck. She didn't want people to talk about the rope mark.

Randall was buried in the Hibdon Cemetery. He was buried toward the back in the new section. Before he was completely covered with dirt, Mrs. Lewis fainted. Mr. Lewis took her home.

When my father returned from the funeral, he talked about Randall. He said Randall was found hanging almost ten feet in the air. A rope was strung from a tree limb and tied to a branch near the ground. They believe he committed suicide. They believed this because his hands weren't tied. He climbed the tree and hung himself. What was unusual was the rope. The rope was new. No one knew where he got the rope.

My mother asked if John Stepp was there. My father said he wasn't. John was where he found Randall. John did not believe he committed suicide. This was when the stories started about John Stepp killing Randall. It was unusual for John to find him. People asked, "Where did he know to look?" There was something strange about the way Randall died. No one believed he hung himself. There was something strange about the way John Stepp found him. No one saw Randall hanging. All they had was John Stepp's word. No one trusted John Stepp. They had to take his word. John Stepp was the constable. His report listed Randall's death as suicide.

The Ghost Woman

It was after dark when Mr. Lewis returned to the Hibdon Cemetery. His wife was real upset and his sister stayed with her. Mr. Lewis wanted to visit his son's grave. He wanted to be alone. The cemetery was a far piece. Mr. Lewis didn't have a car. He walked to the cemetery. The moon had just risen when Mr. Lewis walked through the gate. He walked to where Randall was buried.

The moon was full that night. It rose early. Mr. Lewis didn't have a lantern with him. He had prepared one but he forgot it. He left it on the front porch. It didn't matter. The moon was full and there was a lot of light.

When Mr. Lewis approached his son's grave, he saw something white on it. At first he thought it was flowers, but then, he saw the white thing move. When he got closer, he saw it was a rooster. It was a large, white rooster. The rooster was nesting on his son's grave.

"Get out of there!" Mr. Lewis yelled. He picked up a stick and he started to hit the rooster with the stick. Suddenly, the rooster flew at him. Mr. Lewis fell backward onto the ground. The rooster flapped his wings and jumped at him.

Mr. Lewis rolled away and he quickly stood. The rooster walked back to Randall's grave.

Mr. Lewis held the stick in his hand. He walked toward Randall's grave. "Get out of there!" he yelled. The rooster flew at him again. The rooster flew real high and flapped his wings toward Mr. Lewis' face.

The rooster flew near Mr. Lewis' face. He flapped his wings but he didn't try to spur him. Mr. Lewis was angry. He looked around for a rock and he picked up a small rock. When he threw the rock at the rooster, it struck the fresh dirt on the grave. The rooster moved away when the rock struck the grave.

Mr. Lewis watched the rooster move away from the grave. The rooster moved away real slow. Mr. Lewis walked to his son's grave and he looked at the rooster. The rooster wasn't far from the grave. The rooster stood looking at Mr. Lewis.

It was while Randall's father was standing at the graveside, that he saw the woman. The moon was full and there was a lot of light. He saw her in the corner of his eye. He saw something white behind and to the side of him. He turned to see a woman standing near. She was standing near a tall stone. The stone came almost to her chest. She was wearing a long, white dress and she had long, dark hair.

"Did you know Randall?" Mr. Lewis asked.

The woman didn't say anything.

"Did you know Randall?" Mr. Lewis asked again.

The woman didn't say anything. She began to move around the stone. The woman held to the stone and she moved around it. It looked like she was hugging the stone. She smiled at Mr. Lewis. Then, she began to sway her body. She was dancing!

He watched her dance. She would sway her body and twirl in her dress. The dress was long and it fell to the ground. She didn't make a sound.

The woman danced among the tall stones. She would go behind one and then, stick her head out from behind the stone. She smiled at Mr. Lewis and then she danced in front of it.

"Who are you?" Mr. Lewis asked.

The woman didn't answer. She smiled at Mr. Lewis and slowly danced away. He watched her move away from him and he began to follow her. She danced toward the old section of the cemetery. There were many tall monuments in the old section.

Mr. Lewis followed her. She danced among the stones and she slowly danced away.

He walked toward her. As he walked toward her, she seemed to dance away. He walked a far piece and she kept moving away from him. At one point, she seemed to disappear. He didn't see her! She had danced near several tall monuments. He walked to where he had last seen her but she wasn't there. He had walked to the far end of the cemetery when he heard the noise.

He heard a rooster's wings flapping.

He heard a noise and he turned to look toward his son's grave. He saw her! She was near Randall's grave. He also saw the rooster. The rooster had returned to his son's grave. The woman looked like she was attempting to get to Randall's grave but the rooster was fighting her. Clouds had covered the moon and it was dark. He couldn't see much but it looked like the rooster was flogging the woman with his wings. It looked like the rooster was trying to spur her.

They were fighting!

The woman was attempting to get to Randall's grave and the rooster was fighting her. When she got close to the grave, the rooster would fly at her. She would back away and the rooster returned to Randall's grave. She attempted to get to Randall's grave and the rooster flew at her again. The rooster flew real high and he tried to spur her. When the rooster flew at her, she would back away. She seemed to be afraid of the rooster. One thing was for sure, the rooster wasn't afraid of her. At one point, it looked liked the rooster was chasing her.

Mr. Lewis ran to his son's grave. As he neared the grave, he yelled, "Hay! What are you doing?"

The woman heard his voice and she turned toward him. There was a snarl on her face! Her mouth was turned upward in a snarl. Her hands were held upward as to protect her face. Then, the rooster flogged her again.

Mr. Lewis stopped!

She quickly turned and moved away from Randall's grave. She seemed to dance away. She danced toward several trees and she then went behind the trees. Mr. Lewis followed her. When he came to the trees, she was gone. When he returned to his son's grave, the rooster was nesting. He didn't come near the grave. He walked quickly home.

Randall's father didn't talk about this. He didn't say anything to his wife Georgia. He didn't say anything until they found George.

George Martin is Missing

George Martin was sort of a wild boy. He got into trouble. Not big trouble but he was always doing something. There were times when George would go missing. He would go missing for a day or so. One time, he hitched a ride to Nashville. No one knew why he went to Nashville but he hitched a ride. He had some money on him and a truck driver robbed him. The truck driver beat him up pretty bad. I remember seeing his face at church. He had two black eyes and he could barely walk.

John Stepp went to Nashville to pick him up. A constable found him near the state Capitol. George was beat up real bad. When John Stepp brought him home, George told his father that John Stepp had hit with his gun. George told his father that John Stepp almost broke his arm with that gun. I don't know if people believed George's story but he was beat up pretty bad. No one liked John Stepp and some people believed the story. The story was that John picked up George in Nashville and brought him home. Before they got to Gladeville, John stopped his car and beat up George by the side of the road.

I don't know if the story was true but George seemed to straighten up. He went to church every Sunday and he helped his father with the chores. When he saw John Stepp on the street, George would walk the other way. George didn't like John Stepp. George said, "John Stepp wasn't worth a damn! He never did anything for anybody!"

I wasn't at home when John Stepp came to see my father. I was feeling well so I stayed with my cousin Vera. I spent the night with her. My sister Cleo said John came to our house looking for George. George had been missing for two days. John wanted my father to help him look for George but my father couldn't help. He had a few days of work at the mill. My father had to be at work early.

John Stepp went to a lot of homes. Everyone was busy.

The sun had not set as John drove his car to the Hibdon Cemetery. John had a hunch that he may find George near the Hibdon Cemetery. John wasn't alone in his car. He had a blue tick hound with him. John borrowed one of the Anderson's hunting dogs. He had a shirt that belonged to George and he took the shirt with him.

John stopped his car near the front gate. He turned the engine off and he took the dog from the back seat. He tied a small rope around the dog's neck and he let him smell the shirt.

"Find him!" John said. Then, he let go of the rope.

The dog sniffed the ground then he ran straight for Randall's grave. John followed the dog to the grave. The grave dirt was all messed up. It looked like someone had been digging in the dirt. There was a large hole in the middle. He tied the dog to a small tree and he went back to his car. He opened the trunk and he took out a small shovel.

John returned to Randall's grave and he smoothed it. Then, he let the dog go again.

The dog sniffed around Randall's grave, then he ran toward the old section. John followed him as fast as he could. The dog ran around the tall monuments. John kept following him but the dog was going in circles. The dog kept running around the tall monuments. After a while, John tied the dog.

"He ain't here!" John said to the dog. "What's wrong?"

The dog was real agitated. John let him go again. The dog kept running in circles around the tall monuments. He watched the dog run in circles. John sat down on the ground and he looked at his map. It was while John was looking at the map, that the dog went a different direction.

John wasn't paying much attention until he heard the loud barking. When he looked up, the dog was gone. The barking came from the woods. John dropped the map and ran toward the sound.

He followed the barking. It did not come from where he found Randall. It came from a different direction. He followed the dog's bark. Near a large tree, the dog was barking and jumping upward. When John looked up, he saw George's feet.

The dog was real agitated. He would jump upward then he ran to a tree. There was a rope tied to the tree. The dog sniffed the rope and he went crazy! He would jump upward and howl. The dog kept running around the tree and sniffing the rope. Then, the dog just lay down.

John ran to the dog. His first thought was that a snake had struck him. He looked at the dog but he didn't see any marks. The dog just lay there. He tied him and took him to his car. The dog looked scared, real scared. When John put him in the back seat, the dog peed all over his self.

John returned to the tall monument where he left the map. He walked to where George was hanging and he measured. He calculated how far George was from the rope that was tied. There was still sun. He drew a triangle on the map. George's feet were about ten feet off the ground. When he lowered him, he died the same way Randall died.

Rumors began about John Stepp murdering the two boys. People wondered about the rope. The rope, George was hung with, was the same type of rope Randall was hung with. The rumors didn't start until John started asking questions about the rope. Somehow, people thought John was up to something.

The One Clue

John Stepp walked into the Anderson store. There was one store in town that sold different types of things. When John walked into the store, everybody left. Mr. Anderson was standing behind the counter. He wasn't happy that John Stepp was there. He didn't like John. Several people were shopping. Mrs. Henson had items she was going to purchase. When John Stepp walked into the store, she left the items on the counter and walked out.

"Can I help you?" Mr. Anderson asked.

"I wanted to thank you for letting me borrow your dog. He was real good," John said.

Mr. Anderson grunted. "His name is Bo! He was the best I had! What did you do to him?" he asked.

John was startled. "Nothing! Is something wrong with him?" John asked.

"He's dead!" Mr. Anderson answered.

John walked toward the counter. "I'm real sorry! He acted real funny in the woods and I thought a snake had struck him. I looked at him but there wasn't any mark. I'll pay you for him. Just tell me what he's worth to you," John said.

"He didn't die of snake bite!" Mr. Anderson said.

"How did he die?" John asked.

"He acted real strange when you brought him back. He wouldn't eat. I tied him away from the other dogs because I thought he was sick. I tied him at the privy. About sunrise, he began to howl real loud. When I went to check him, he was dead!" Mr. Anderson replied.

"What can I do for you?" he added.

John walked toward the counter and he leaned on it. "I'm real sorry about your dog," he said. "I'll take him to Nashville and have a vet look at him if you think he was sick."

"He's already buried. What can I do for you?" Mr. Anderson repeated.

John had a small cloth bag in his hand. He opened the bag and he laid a short length of rope on the counter. "You have probably heard that Randall and George hung themselves. They were both hung with the same type of rope," he said. "I wanted to know if you sold them the rope."

Mr. Anderson moved away from the counter. "Are you saying I had something to do with those boys dying?" he asked.

"No. I just wanted to know if you sold them the rope. I wanted to know when you sold it," John replied.

Mr. Anderson walked to the counter and he picked up the rope. He looked at it very carefully. He held it in his hands and he walked to one of the counters. He picked up a knife from a shelf and he attempted to cut the rope. He couldn't. Mr. Anderson used several knives from his shelf. None of the knives would cut the rope. He picked up a straight razor. The razor cut the rope. He looked where he had cut it. "It's not mine!" he said. "I have never sold this type of rope."

"What kind of rope is it?" John asked.

Mr. Anderson walked to the counter and he placed the length of rope in front of John. "I don't know! I have never seen anything like it!" he said.

"What are you talking about?" John asked.

Mr. Anderson walked toward the back of his store. There were several coils of rope hanging on the wall. He took one and brought it back to the counter. He held it up to John's face. "The rope I sell is made of hemp. The strands are short. They are short because short strands are cheaper to use," he said.

He picked up the length of rope he had cut. "These strands are long and thick. The longer and thicker the strand, the stronger the rope," he added.

"How strong is it?" John asked.

Mr. Anderson looked at the length of rope. "From the looks of this rope, the strands may be two to three feet. They are intertwined," he said. He placed the rope on the counter. "My guess is this rope could lift that car you drive," he added.

"Is there anything else I can help you with?" Mr. Anderson asked.

"Yes! Where do you buy your rope?" John asked.

Mr. Anderson was startled by the question. His first impression was that John Stepp didn't believe him when he told him he didn't sell that rope. He became agitated and nervous. "I buy it from a salesman out of Nashville," he answered.

"Where does he get it?" John asked.

Mr. Anderson was real nervous. He gulped, "He buys it from Acme Wholesalers in Memphis."

"Does all the rope come from Memphis?" John asked.

Mr. Anderson was real nervous. "Everything I sell comes from Memphis. Everything comes from Acme Wholesalers," he replied.

"I'm sorry about your dog. He did a real fine job," John Stepp said. He turned and walked out of the store.

John Stepp left Anderson's store and he walked to his office. Before he unlocked the door, he checked his mailbox. There were several letters. John checked the letters carefully. He looked at the postmark. He was looking for a letter postmarked from Memphis. There were none.

John unlocked the door and he went in. The stove was cold and the coffee was cold. John poured a cup of cold coffee. He sat at his desk and he looked at a map lying on his desk. He didn't look at the map he looked at two triangles he had drawn on the map. The triangles were of the distance and length of the rope that was used to hang Randall and George.

He took a sheet of paper and he began to calculate. He calculated distance and weight. He calculated how strong the rope must have been and how much strength it would take to hang both boys. The calculations didn't make any sense.

After a while, John took off his hat and coat. He removed his gun from his coat and he placed it on the desk. He turned the oil lamp low and he went to sleep.

The Letters

John had spent most of the day near the Hibdon Cemetery. He had visited the area where he found Randall and George. It was late and John returned to his office. He checked his mailbox and there were several letters. One was from the Sheriff in Lebanon. One was postmarked from Memphis. He unlocked the door and entered.

He went immediately to his desk and he opened the letter from the Sheriff. It was short.

September 18, 1928

Constable Stepp,

Your trip is approved.

Craig Lawson
Office of the Sheriff of Wilson County

John opened the letter postmarked from Memphis. The letter was short.

September 12, 1928

Constable Stepp,
I received your package. How soon can you get here?

R. B. - Acme Wholesalers
Memphis, Tennessee

John stood and he walked to the door. When he left, he didn't lock it. He walked to the Texaco filling station.

Brandon was sitting inside when John walked in. "Do you have it?" he asked.

Brandon jumped up very quickly. "Yes! I have it! It came two days ago!" he answered.

"Do you have the cans?" John asked.

Brandon saluted John. "Yes sir!" he replied. "When do you need them?" he asked.

"I don't know!" John responded. "Just have everything ready," he said.

Abram's Visit

Nothing happened the next few weeks. I wasn't too ill and I went to school. I liked school. My teacher was Miss. Sally. Miss. Sally was older and she wasn't married. She was always very nice to me. When the other kids went outside to play Miss. Sally would help me with my spelling words. I was real far behind the other kids but nobody made fun of me. I guess everyone knew I had been sick and they understood.

My sister Cleo helped me a lot. We didn't have electricity we used coal oil lamps. Cleo would help me at the eating table. She would set with me and help me with my reading. It was while Cleo was helping me with my reading one night that Abram came to see my father. I don't know why he came but he did.

Abram knocked on our door and my father answered the knock. When he opened the door, Abram was standing there. "I need to talk to you Mr. Singer. It's important," he said.

Abram came into our house and he sat in a chair. "I don't know if you know but several months ago, John Stepp threatened to kill Randall and George," he said.

We were all shocked to hear that.

"What are you talking about?" my father asked Abram.

Abram took a deep breath. He looked scared. "Do you remember when Miss. Agnes' cow wandered off? Well, the cow didn't wander off,

Randall, George, and me, we," Abram stopped talking and he took a deep breath. "We pulled a prank on Miss. Agnes. We hid her cow in the woods."

My father looked at my mother. He had an angry look on his face. "That cow was tied to a tree. If John Stepp hadn't found her, she would have died tied to that tree. John looked all day for that cow. Why did you do that?" my father asked.

Abram took a deep breath. He stood and looked toward the door. "I don't know. We were just having fun. That don't excuse what John Stepp did to us," he said.

"What did John Stepp do to you?" my father asked.

Abram turned around very quickly. "He must of figured we did it!" he said. "John Stepp came and got us. He took us to his office and locked us up. He sat in a chair near the jail door and he cleaned his gun. He didn't say anything for a while. He just cleaned his gun."

My father looked at my mother. "That don't sound like he threatened to kill you," he said.

Abram sat down in the chair. He looked at my father. "He did!" he said. "John Stepp started talking about Miss. Agnes. He said she was a widow and that she was real upset about her cow. He said there

were a lot of old folks and they don't need that kind
of worry. Then, he pointed his gun at us."

"We were real scared. John Stepp pointed his
gun at us. He told us if we ever did anything like
that again, he would take us to the woods," he
added.

"What happened then?" my father asked.

Abram stood. He wrung his hands together. "He
told us it was late and our folks may be worried.
Then, he let us go," Abram said.

"Why do you think John killed Randall and
George?" my father asked.

"Because they both wound up dead in the
woods. I think John Stepp took them to the woods
and hung them," Abram said. "I think I'm next!"
Abram sat down in the chair.

My father looked at my mother. "John Stepp has
done a lot of things but I don't recall him ever killing
anybody. Why would John want to kill you boys?"
he asked.

Abram was real nervous. He stood again and he
wrung his hands together. "I don't know," he said.
"John beat up George once and he threatened to kill
us. I think someone needs to go to the Sheriff and
have John Stepp arrested!"

"Arrested for what?" my father asked.

Abram yelled real loud, "Arrested for killing Randall and George! They didn't hang themselves! John Stepp murdered them! He took them to the woods and he murdered them!"

We just looked at Abram. I don't think my mother and father knew what to say. Then, Abram began to cry.

My father stood and he put his arms around Abram. "Let's go home," he said. My father held to Abram and he walked him home.

Abram visited a lot of people the next few days. He told them the same story. He told people that John Stepp had put them in jail and pointed his gun at them. He said John Stepp threatened to kill them.

I think my father believed Abram because he didn't like John Stepp. He was afraid of him. My mother and father argued about what Abram had said. I didn't know. I only knew that I didn't like John Stepp and two boys were dead.

Stories of Ghosts

Nothing much happened until the night of the new moon. I was feeling better and I went to church. Reverend King talked about the Holy Ghost and about people dying and going to heaven. He talked about Randall and George. He said they were in heaven with the Lord. When the service was over we went outside. There was a small crowd of people standing and talking. Abram was talking to several of the men. We wanted to hear what he was saying so we walked to them.

"She is no ghost!" Abram said. "Randall, George, and I saw her several times. She lives in Smyrna and she is crazy!"

"I saw her!" Mr. Lewis said. "She was trying to get to Randall's grave and that rooster tried to spur her!"

The men were laughing at Mr. Lewis.

"Randall was a good boy," Mr. Lewis said. "He is in heaven because he was good. That ghost woman did something real bad! The Lord won't let her into heaven."

Abram laughed. "What did the rooster do? Did the rooster do something real bad also?" he asked.

The men laughed.

"I saw her!" Mr. Lewis said. "She was trying to get to Randall's grave and the rooster fought her. I saw her dancing and then she disappeared behind some trees."

The men laughed.

Abram got real serious. "We saw her! We saw her dancing several times," Abram said. "George said he heard somebody say they saw a ghost woman dancing in the cemetery. We didn't believe in ghosts but we wanted to see. George, Randall, and I sneaked out one night and we saw her. We never saw a rooster. She is as real as you and me. We almost caught her once! We separated and went at her from several directions. Somehow she slipped by us."

"She is no ghost! She is a crazy woman!" he added.

Mr. Jackson was standing near Abram. "If she is crazy, why did you want to catch her?" he asked. "All women are crazy!"

The men just laughed.

"Let's go tonight!" Mr. Jackson said. He pointed toward his wife. "I have seen a lot of crazy women but I never saw one dance in a graveyard."

The men laughed.

Mr. Lewis was angry. "She is a ghost!" he said.

Abram laughed, "The woman isn't a ghost! She's real! It's the rooster that's a ghost!"

The men laughed.

The Late Night Vigil

The story began to spread about the ghost woman and the men began to talk about her. That night, several of the men went to the graveyard. They waited to see her. They arrived after sunset.

The men were waiting by the gate of the Hibdon Cemetery when they heard John Stepp's car. They heard that fender rattling. John drove up to the gate and he got out of his car. He didn't turn the engine off.

"What are you men doing?" John asked.

"Were waiting for the ghost woman," Mr. Jackson said.

John Stepp laughed. He laughed real hard. The men were surprised to hear John laugh. I don't think anyone ever heard John Stepp laugh.

"It's a prank," John said. He went to the trunk of his car and he took a lantern from it and he lit it. It was a new moon and it was dark. He turned the car engine off and he looked around the men. He was looking for Abram. Abram wasn't there.

"Did Abram tell you there was a ghost woman in the cemetery?" he asked.

Mr. Lewis stepped forward. "No! I did!" he said.

John pointed his lantern toward Mr. Lewis. "Hello, Mr. Lewis," he said. "I'm sorry about Randall."

John held his lantern real high. "There are no ghosts! When you die you go to heaven or hell. If you go to heaven, you don't want to come back. If you go to hell, you can't come back," he said.

The men laughed.

Mr. Lewis stepped forward. "It isn't funny!" he said. "I saw her! She was trying to get to Randall's grave and a rooster tried to spur her."

The men laughed.

John Stepp didn't laugh. "Where did you see her?" he asked Mr. Lewis.

Mr. Lewis pointed toward Randall's grave. "I came here the night Randall was buried. There was a rooster nesting on his grave and I drove him away. Then I saw the ghost woman," Mr. Lewis paused. "She tried to get to Randall's grave and the rooster fought her. I followed her but she disappeared."

Mr. Lewis pointed toward the far end of the cemetery. "She disappeared there," he added.

John pointed his lantern toward Randall's grave. "I'll take a look," he said.

John Stepp started walking toward Randall's grave. He stopped and turned around. "Anybody want to join me?" he asked.

The men nodded their heads no.

John turned and he walked toward Randall's grave. There was a new moon and it was dark. John pointed his lantern toward the graves. He walked past Randall's grave to where George was buried. When he came to George's grave, he shined the lantern on it. Someone had been digging. The grave had been disturbed and there was a large hole.

John turned and he walked to Randall's grave. When he came to Randall's grave he shined the lantern on it. The grave had been disturbed. Someone had been digging. There was a large hole in the center.

John began to walk to several of the graves. He shined his lantern on them. He was looking for signs of someone digging. They were not disturbed. He walked to where Mr. Lewis said the ghost woman disappeared. There were several tall monuments and trees. The trees were at the far end of the cemetery. He shined his lantern on the trees. There was nothing.

He looked toward the men. They were far away. He could see their lanterns. He looked to the left, that is the direction he found Randall. He looked toward the right, that is the direction he found George. John shined his lantern in all directions. He stood for a minute. Then, he walked back to the men.

"I didn't see anything," John said. He looked at Mr. Lewis. "Did you ever give anything of value to Randall like a watch?" he asked.

Mr. Lewis was puzzled by the question. "I have a pocket watch that belonged to my father," he answered.

"Is it a gold watch?" John asked.

Mr. Lewis was puzzled. "No! It's silver. I have it at the house if you want to see it. Did you find a gold watch on Randall?" he asked.

"No," John replied. "I was just wondering if you may have given a gold watch to Randall."

"Is something wrong?" Mr. Jackson asked. "Did someone lose a gold watch?"

"No. I have not heard of anyone losing a watch," John answered. "Let's go home! I didn't see any ghost woman or rooster."

The men turned and they began to walk in different directions. When John saw their lanterns far down the road, he opened the trunk of his car. He took out a hammer and a shovel. He walked to George's grave and he began to dig.

John had dug down near six feet when he struck the pine box. He moved enough dirt away to use the hammer to open it. When he opened it, the smell was real bad. George had not been embalmed. He shined his lantern on George's body. As far as he could tell, the body had not been disturbed. John checked George's pockets. There was nothing there. He closed the lid and hammered the nails back in. He replaced the dirt and smoothed the top. Then, he went to Randall's grave.

The sun was almost up when John replaced the dirt on Randall's grave. Neither body had been disturbed. There was nothing in their pockets. Someone had been digging on their graves. Someone had tried to dig them up. He returned the shovel and hammer to his car and he took out his map. He walked to George's grave and he walked to where he had found him. He marked the map with a pencil. Then, he walked to Randall's grave. He drew lines on the map where he found them and where they were buried.

John was tired. He had been up all night. He rested a minute then he began walking around the cemetery. He looked at each grave to see if someone had been digging. He found nothing. The only graves that had been disturbed were Randall and George's. John also looked for any sign of a rooster. He walked all around Randall's grave looking for feathers. If a rooster had tried to spur someone, there should be feathers. There weren't. He looked for droppings. There were none.

It was nine o'clock when John left the cemetery. That night he returned. He parked his car near the old county road and he walked to the cemetery. He sat near the spot Mr. Lewis said he saw the ghost woman disappear. He sat and waited. John had a lantern with him but he didn't light it. He sat and waited. His gun lay beside him. Beside his gun was a gun belt loaded with shells.

People began to talk about the ghost woman and they tried to guess who she was. Miss. Agnes said it was Johnnie Lee. Johnnie Lee was about nineteen when she died. She died many years ago from eating poisoned poke salad. She died and she was buried in the Hibdon Cemetery. One day, I was feeling pretty good. My mother and father took us to the Hibdon Cemetery. We looked for Johnnie Lee's grave. My father found it. She died in 1901.

The stories of the ghost woman seemed to fade away. No one saw her. John Stepp went to the cemetery several times to wait for her. Perhaps he did not go at the right time. It seemed she only appeared when the moon was full. John didn't believe in her. I didn't believe in her either. I didn't believe in her until I saw her.

Andy

I was getting ill again. I had missed several weeks of school. One night, I heard a sound on the roof of our house. At first, it sounded like rain. Then, I realized it was our rooster. I could hear him on our roof. The sound of a rooster crowing woke me. When I heard his crow, I saw the first light of morning come through my window. Then, I realized it wasn't our rooster. The crow was real loud. It sounded like a victory call.

I kept hearing the sound of the rooster on our roof for several nights. Then, I heard it outside my window. A rooster was walking on our porch. I would hear him walk back and forth. At first light, he crowed. The crow woke me. When I heard the crow, the first light of morning came through my window.

One night, I heard the sound of the rooster on our porch. I was feeling better and I looked out the window. There on our porch was a large, white rooster. The rooster was walking back and forth on our porch. I got up and went outside.

The rooster came right to me. He was real pretty. I sat and talked to him. I don't know if he knew what I said but he let me touch him and he let me pick him up. I sat in one of our chairs and talked to him. He just sat in my lap and let me pet him. I gave him a name. The name I gave him was Andrew. Andrew was one of the apostles. He didn't seem to like that name so I shortened it to Andy. He seemed to like the name Andy.

I never saw him during the daytime. He only came at night. The sun would set and Andy would appear. When the sun began to rise, Andy would crow. Then he went somewhere. We never saw him during the day.

Andy was pretty for a rooster. He was large and white. He didn't look like our rooster because he was always clean. He was white like a cloud or new fallen snow. He smelled good too! Andy smelled like a flower or perfume or something. I had never smelled anything like it. He would let me hold him. He would set in my lap and let me stroke his comb.

There was something strange about Andy. He never fought our rooster. Usually two roosters will fight. My father was afraid Andy would fight our rooster but he didn't. Andy had two spurs on each leg. Our rooster only had one on each leg. Andy's four spurs were long and razor sharp. I had heard of people fighting roosters near Murfreesboro. My father said if Andy ever fought another rooster he would win. Those spurs were sharp like a razor. If Andy spurred another rooster, he would cut the other rooster to pieces.

Andy never bothered our chickens and he never bothered our rooster. One night, our rooster came up on our front porch. I was sitting in a chair holding Andy and our rooster walked all around us. He never looked at Andy. Our rooster seemed to ignore him. Our rooster acted like Andy wasn't there.

When Randall's father heard about Andy, he came to our house to see him. He wanted to see if Andy was the same rooster that he saw fighting the ghost woman. Randall's father didn't know. The rooster he saw was mean. The rooster tried to stop him from getting near his son's grave. Andy was gentle. He let Mr. Lewis pet him. Andy was my pet.

It was during the church hayride that I saw the ghost woman. I was still ill but I wanted to go on the hayride. My mother wrapped me in a blanket and we went to the church. It was dark when we got to the church. I had not seen Andy. He usually showed up at our house when the sun went down. I looked for him and called for him but he didn't come. When we got to the church, Andy was there.

When I saw Andy, he came right to me. He let me pick him up. I held on to him and my father sat me on the wagon.

We all got on the wagon and I sat at the back. Andy was setting in my lap. The moon was full as we began to slowly go down the road. We were all singing and having a good time when we neared the Hibdon Cemetery. When we neared the cemetery, Andy began to act funny. He seemed agitated.

The night was clear but a light rain began to fall. I think it was the rain that made me ill again. I didn't get real wet but I did get wet. When we neared the cemetery, we saw her! A woman was dancing among the graves. She was wearing a white dress and she looked young.

Everyone was quite. We could hear the clip clop of the horse's hoofs on the dirt road. The wagon went slowly past the cemetery. The woman danced from the graves to the road. She began to dance behind the wagon. I looked at her but I didn't think she was a ghost. She looked like a woman dancing on the road. We thought it was a prank. We thought someone did this to scare us.

I was sitting in the back with my feet dangling down and Andy was sitting in my lap. The woman kept dancing behind the wagon. Closer and closer she came. I sat looking at her. She came close, real close. She was wearing a long, white dress that went to the ground. The dress was not a nightgown but a real pretty white dress. It was simple. The dress tied at the bodice. I couldn't see her feet. I remember looking toward her feet to see what kind of shoes she was wearing. I couldn't see her feet. Her dress went all the way to the ground.

She was real pretty! She wasn't very tall. I couldn't see through her dress but I could see her body move against it. She was thin. She had an even body. Her hair was long and black. Her face was real even and small. Her eyes were real dark. I couldn't tell what color they were because they were dark. Her eyes were wide. I remember looking at her skin. Her skin wasn't white it was tanned. Her skin was a light brown color.

She wasn't wearing any kind of makeup. Her lips were full and pink. I could see her hands. Her fingernails were long and white. The fingernails did not have any color on them.

She was beautiful!

I saw her face smile. She had a beautiful smile. Her teeth were very white and even. She danced behind the wagon and she reached out to touch my foot when Andy attacked her.

Andy flew out of my lap. His wings were flapping. The woman stopped dancing. She and Andy were standing in the road. When the woman tried to pass him, he flew at her. She was afraid of Andy. I watched them fight. The ghost woman and Andy were fighting in the road.

The driver sped the horses and we moved quickly away. I didn't see Andy any more that night. I was afraid for him. It was near sunrise when I heard him. I heard Andy crow. It was real loud. It was a victory yell.

People began talking about the ghost woman. One day, John Stepp came to our house to ask about her. It seemed many people had seen her. I remember John Stepp asking me about her. He asked a lot of questions. Some of the questions I didn't understand.

"What did she look like?" John asked.

"She was real pretty," I answered.

"Did she touch you?" he asked.

"No," I answered.

"Could you see through her?" he asked.

"No," I answered.

"Why did the rooster attack her?" he asked.

"I don't know. It looked like she was going to grab my foot," I answered.

"Did she make any faces at you?" he asked.

"No. She smiled real pretty," I answered.

"Could you see through her?" he asked.

"No," I answered.

"Did she look like anyone you know?" he asked.

"No. I have never seen her," I answered.

"Did the rooster try to spur her?" he asked.

"Yes," I answered.

John Stepp stood and he walked away from me. He paused a minute and he turned around. "Did she any kind of scar or mark on her?" he asked.

"What do you mean?" I asked.

John pointed to his face. "Did she have any kind of scar?" he asked again.

"No," I answered.

John came to me and he got real close. "Do you believe in ghosts?" he asked.

"No," I answered.

"Why?" John asked.

"She didn't look like a ghost. She looked like a woman dancing in the road," I answered.

John stood and he looked at my mother. My mother wasn't touched that day because she was real polite to John Stepp. She smiled at him. "Where is the rooster?" John asked.

"I don't know," my mother answered.

John turned to me and leaned down real close. "That rooster must be real brave to fight that woman. Where is he? I would like to thank him," he said.

"I don't know," I answered.

John looked puzzled. He stood and looked at my mother. "We only see him at night," my mother said. "We have never seen him in the daytime."

John looked real puzzled. "He must nest somewhere," he said.

"I don't know where he is. Jay looked for him once but he never found him. When the sun goes down, we see him. He walks around our porch and he lets Sarah Jane hold him. We hear him crow when the sun comes up. We see him at night. We have never seen him in the daylight," my mother answered.

"Can I look for him?" John asked.

My mother got touched because she had a frown on her face. I think she thought John Stepp was calling her a liar. She shrugged her shoulders. "Look all you like! You won't find him! He only comes at night," she said.

John stayed a while. He looked everywhere for Andy. He climbed in our attic. Our attic was only a small crawl space but he looked there. He looked everywhere. He went to our hen house and he checked our barn.

It was late in the day when John Stepp left our house. He thanked my mother and me for answering his questions. He said he was going into town to eat. Supper was almost ready and we had plenty. My mother didn't invite John Stepp to stay. My mother didn't like John Stepp.

John ate his ham sandwich and drank his coffee. He had been at the diner for sometime. Many people came, ate, and left. John sat near the back. He had a map laid out on the table and he had been studying it. He had some paper and he kept writing on the paper. Miss. Louise would watch him and make motions. She would point toward her head and make a rotating motion with her finger. When people saw her hand make the motion, they would laugh.

John didn't notice the laughter. He kept looking at the map. He didn't notice anything, including the time.

"I need to lock up!" Mr. Benson said. Mr. Benson was the owner of the diner. John didn't notice what he said. Mr. Benson walked real close to John. "I need to lock up!" he said loudly. John looked up at Mr. Benson. He had an angry look on his face.

Mr. Benson backed away from the table and he lowered his voice. "It's real late. I need to lock up," he said.

John reached into his pocket and he looked at his watch. The time was ten o'clock. "Sorry," John said. "I didn't realize how late it was."

Miss. Louise came to the table. "You have been here since five! When do you sleep?" she asked.

John didn't answer. He rolled up the map and he took his paper. When he stood up, he looked at Mr. Benson. John had an angry look on his face. "Sorry! I didn't realize how late it was," he said.

The door was locked and Mr. Benson opened it to let John leave. John walked to his office. He checked his mail before he opened the door. There were several letters. One letter was postmarked from Memphis.

The office was dark and John lit a lamp on his desk. He took off his coat. Before he took off his coat, he removed his gun. He laid his gun on his desk and he sat in the chair. There was cup of cold coffee on the desk and he finished what was left.

He opened the letter postmarked from Memphis and he read it. It was very short. When he began to read it, John laughed. It wasn't a small laugh it was a belly laugh. John read the letter and he laughed.

September 14, 1928

John,

I received your letter. I don't know if I can help you but I will do what I can. I got the medicine for the little girl. The doctor gave me several doses. It needs to be mixed with whiskey. Can you get a bottle?

Looking forward to seeing you again. Do you still have that sawed-off shotgun?

Yours truly,

Oliver

John read the letter and he laughed. He removed his hat. Before he went to sleep, he locked the door and placed his gun near his bed.

The Experiment

Mr. Jones heard the sound of John Stepp's car as he sat at the eating table. He could hear that fender rattling. He expected the car to keep driving but it stopped in front of his house. He heard the engine turn off. Mr. Jones knew it was John Stepp stopping at his house but he didn't go to the door. Mr. Jones sat at the table until he heard a knock at the door. When he opened it, John Stepp was standing there.

"I'm sorry to disturb you Mr. Jones but I would like to speak to your son Michael," John said.

"What has he done?" Mr. Jones asked.

"Nothing. I wanted to speak to him. I wanted him to do something for me," John replied.

"Do what?" Mr. Jones asked.

"Your son is about the same age as Randall and George. I have seen him and he looks pretty spry. I wanted to see if he could climb a tree," John answered.

"What tree?" Mr. Jones asked.

"Could you come outside Mr. Jones?" John asked.

Mr. Jones followed John Stepp outside. They walked to John's car. "I want to see if Michael can climb the tree that George hung himself on. I wanted to see how much effort it would have taken," John said.

Mr. Jones looked away from John. He didn't like John and he heard the stories about John beating up George. He looked toward his house. "I don't want Michael mixed up in this," Mr. Jones said.

"I just want to try a experiment. It won't take long. I'll pay him," John said.

Mr. Jones looked at John. "How much?" he asked.

"I think I can get him a dollar," John replied.

Mr. Jones' face lit up. "A dollar to climb a tree? What if he can't do it?" he asked.

"He gets the dollar whether he can climb it or not," John answered.

"When do you want him?" Mr. Jones asked.

"I'm going there now! How soon can he get there?" John asked.

"I'll have there in one hour," Mr. Jones replied.

John started to crank his car when he stopped and looked at Mr. Jones. He had a real stern look on his face. "This is official business! The county will pay Michael. I would appreciate it if you didn't say anything," John said.

Mr. Jones got a big smile on his face. "Climbing a tree for a dollar is one thing. Asking me to keep quite about this is another," Mr. Jones said. "That will cost fifty cents!"

John Stepp smiled. When Mr. Jones saw John smile he backed away. He had never seen John Stepp smile. He saw John reach into his coat pocket. The first thing Mr. Jones thought was John was going to kill him. John was going to shoot him with that gun that shot dimes. Mr. Jones' heart almost stopped.

John pulled a wallet out of his coat. He opened it and he handed Mr. Jones a dollar. "Thank you," he said.

Mr. Jones looked at the dollar. "I don't have any money! I don't have any change!" he said.

John cranked his car and he got in.

Mr. Jones walked to the driver's side. "I don't have any change!" he said.

John looked at Mr. Jones. There was a smile on his face. "There is no change! Fifty cents a tree is fair. Michael will get one dollar for each tree," he said smiling.

When John arrived at the Hibdon Cemetery, Michael was waiting for him. Michael was out of breath. He must of ran all they way and took a short cut through the woods. When John pulled up to the gate, Michael ran to the car.

"Mr. Stepp, I'm ready! I can climb anything! Just show me the trees!" he said breathing heavily.

"Rest a bit! I don't think it will take long!" John said.

"When do I get the money?" Michael asked.

"It may take a few weeks but I think I can advance it to you now," John replied. He handed Michael two one-dollar bills.

Michael looked at the money. He was excited. "Two dollars!" he said.

John turned off the car engine and he took a map from the trunk of his car. He had a long coil of rope. It wasn't the rope used to hang Randall and George it was smaller in diameter. He handed the rope to Michael. "Wait here!" he said.

John took the map and he walked toward the far end of the cemetery. He walked to Randall's grave first. He looked at the grave; it had not been disturbed. He then walked to George's grave. When he looked at it, someone had been digging. There was a large hole in the center. John looked back toward Michael. Michael was sitting beside his car. He looked at the grave again. He noticed something in the dirt.

John walked to his car. "This is official business! I don't want you talking to anyone about anything you see or hear," John said.

Michael smiled. "Climbing two trees is one thing! Keeping quite about it is something different!" he said. Michael held his hand out.

John smiled and he reached into his coat pocket. He handed Michael a one-dollar bill. "This way," John said.

The first tree wasn't far from the cemetery. This was the tree he found Randall hanging from. When they arrived, Michael had a surprised look on his face. Everything was marked. There were stakes in the ground and a rope was tied to a low tree limb. The rope went upward to a large limb. Then, it came downward to a spot on the ground. The rope was staked.

"You're not to tell anyone what you see or hear," John ordered.

Michael nodded his head.

John took the rope from Michael and he threw one end over a large limb. He handed the other end to Michael. "I don't want you to fall! Tie this around your waist," John ordered.

Michael tied the rope around his waist. John took his pocket watch from his coat pocket. He pointed upward into the tree. He pointed to where a rope went around the tree and then to the ground. "You have five minutes to climb to that limb. Take your time. I want to see how far you can get in five minutes. If you get scared, climb down," he ordered.

Michael climbed about one-third of the way until he got stuck. The tree limbs were far apart and he had difficulty reaching one. Michael was about the same height as Randall. George was a little shorter. John concluded Randall could not have climbed that tree.

Michael climbed down and they went to the other tree. Michael was surprised; this tree was staked out the same way. There was rope tied to a low limb. The rope went upward to a large limb. It went downward to the ground and it was staked. John threw the rope over a limb and he handed one end to Michael. Michael tied the end to his waist.

Michael started to climb the tree and John stopped him. "Wait for my watch hand to come around. Take your time. I want to see how far you can get in five minutes," he said.

"Now!" John said. Michael climbed that tree like a squirrel. In two minutes, he was half way up. In three minutes he was near the limb. Then, he stopped. "I can't make it!" Michael yelled. "There's nothing to hold on to."

"Come down!" John ordered.

John looked at his watch. There was no way either boy could have climbed the tree and then hung his self. He figured if it took longer than five minutes, they would have backed out.

"I see something!" Michael yelled.

John looked upward. Michael was still sitting near the limb. "I see a rope hanging from a tree limb," he yelled.

"Where?" John yelled. He began to look in different directions.

"Wait! It is the rope from the other tree! I can see the other tree from here," Michael yelled.

"Are you sure!" John yelled.

"Yes sir!" Michael yelled. "I remember that limb I couldn't reach. I can also see partially where you staked it."

"Look around! See if you see anything else! I don't care what it is. Look for something that doesn't belong," John ordered.

Michael looked all around. He could see a far piece. He could see the cemetery and John Stepp's car. He could see the graves of Randall and George. He knew where they were because he came to their funeral. Michael didn't see anything out of place. He didn't see anything that didn't belong but he did notice something. He climbed down.

"Mr. Stepp, you paid me one dollar not to tell anyone anything I saw or heard. How much will you pay me for something I noticed?" Michael asked.

John looked at Michael. He didn't see the humor in Michael's question. He looked at him sternly. "It depends on what you noticed," John said.

"I don't know. It could be important! I won't tell anybody! Honest!" Michael said.

"What is it?" John asked.

"I didn't notice it at first," Michael said. "I didn't notice it from the first tree. I noticed it from the second tree." Michael paused.

John looked at Michael. He had a real stern look on his face. "What did you notice?" John asked.

Michael took a deep breath. "I noticed how far away from everything this cemetery is. I could see the graves and the road. I could see your car near the gate," he said. "This cemetery hasn't been used in many years. I could see Randall and George's graves. I noticed them because I knew about where they were and I could see a color difference in the ground. I could see that the dirt was fresh."

John was worried that Michael had seen the hole in George's grave. "What did you notice about the dirt?" John asked.

"The color difference!" Michael answered. "The new graves are dark and the old ones are light. George's grave is newer than Randall's grave so it looks darker. They are both dark compared to the others."

Michael took another deep breath. "I didn't notice how thick the trees were until I climbed the second tree," he said. "I noticed there were a lot of branches and that there were a lot of leaves. I noticed that the sap had spotted the limbs and the leaves." Michael held up his hands toward John. "There is sap on the tree. I got it on my hands!"

John was irritated. "What did you notice Michael?" he asked.

Michael took a deep breath. "I noticed that I knew where to look. I was real high and I knew where the cemetery was and I knew where the gate was. I was real high," he said.

John was puzzled. "What are you talking about?" John asked.

Michael looked real sad. He lowered his head then he looked up at John. "Mr. Stepp, what I noticed was that I was real high and everything else was low. What I noticed was that no one would have ever found them. Not even in the wintertime.

The trees are real thick. No one could have seen them from the cemetery or the gate. No one would have ever found them," he said.

Michael lowered his head. "Mr. Stepp, they would have just hung there. No one would have ever found them," he repeated.

John stood for a moment. He looked around where they were standing. Michael was correct! If he hadn't looked for them, when he did, no one would have found them. He found Randall by accident. If he had a waited a few days, he would not have smelled where Randall soiled his pants when he was hung. There would have been no smell. Over a period of days, the tree sap would spot the rope and their bodies. The new rope would begin to look like the tree. The rope would look like a vine. Their bodies would begin to look like the trees.

It never occurred to him look up. If there had been men helping him, they would have walked past them. He would not have found George if he had not found Randall.

What Michael noticed was important. Someone went to a great deal of effort to hide their bodies. Someone didn't want them found. Randall and George were murdered. The question was why. The big question was who did it.

John placed his hand on Michael's shoulder. "This is official business!" he said. "What you noticed is worth two dollars. You are not to tell anyone what you saw, heard, or noticed."

John reached into his coat pocket. He opened his wallet and he gave Michael four dollars. Michael took the money. "This is four dollars. You said two," Michael said.

"Two dollars per tree! If you hadn't climbed the first tree, you wouldn't have noticed what you did from the second tree," John answered.

"Can I go home?" Michael asked.

"Yes! I am going to stay a while," John replied.

John walked Michael to the gate of the cemetery. He watched Michael slowly walk away. When Michael was far down the road, John opened the trunk of his car and he took a shovel from the trunk. He walked to George's grave.

The dirt was disturbed like the last time. John placed the shovel on the ground and he looked real close. He thought he saw something earlier and he did. There was an impression in the dirt. He looked carefully. There was more than one. John took his pencil and he measured one of the impressions. At one point, he looked at his left hand. He measured his left hand with the pencil.

John returned to where he left his map. He had left his map where he found George. When John picked up the map, he noticed a spot of sap. He looked upward. It was summer. Michael was correct. The summer sap would have covered most of everything. They would never have found them. He marked the map with the measurements he had taken. John returned to George's grave and he began digging.

He dug about five feet when he realized whoever was digging did not go further than three feet. The dirt was hard and undisturbed. Whoever tried to dig up George was stopped. They were stopped twice. Something stopped them from digging. They never got further than three feet.

Abram is Missing

Many things happened before the next moon. The next moon was a special moon. It was like a harvest moon, but different. It was called the double moon. There appeared to be two moons when there was only one.

It was during this time, before the double moon, that Abram disappeared. I was very ill when I heard the loud knock on our door. It was late, very late.

Bamm! Bamm! Bamm! The door shook as someone pounded on it.

"Wake Up Jay!" a loud voice called out.

Bamm! Bamm! Bamm! The door shook.

My father woke up and put his pants on. As he was putting his pants on, my mother lit an oil lamp. The noise woke me. I sat up in the bed. I could hear the pounding on the door.

My father opened the door to see John Stepp. "Abram is missing! You're a special deputy!" John yelled. "Where are your shoes?"

My father was holding his boots in his hand. John grabbed him by the collar of his shirt and pulled him outside. "Get in the truck!" he ordered.

"What are you doing?" my mother yelled.

"Abrams missing!" John yelled. "These men are special deputies."

My mother looked outside. There was a large truck. It was dark but she could see the outline of several men in the back. There were small gates around the truck and she could see the outline of the men.

"Get in!" John ordered my father. He looked at my mother and he tipped his hat. "Sorry mam! I need Jay to help me look for Abram. He'll get paid," John said.

My father hobbled to the truck as he was trying to get his boots on. John walked to him and he picked up like a sack of potatoes. John pushed him into the truck. Then, the truck sped away.

Jay was trying to get his boots on when he looked around. All of the men were there. The men stood quiet. They didn't say anything.

"You can't do this," Jay said.

"Yes I can!" John yelled. "Abrams missing and I need you to help me search."

"I got a job at the mill. If I'm not at work, Harold will fire me," Jay pleaded.

"Harold won't fire you," John yelled. He looked at the men. "Abrams missing! We're going to search the woods near the Hibdon Cemetery."

"You got to let me go!" Jay pleaded. "Sarah Jane is sick. I need the money!"

"You'll get paid!" John said. He looked at the men. "You are all special deputies. The county will pay you!"

"You don't understand," Jay pleaded. "If I'm not at work, Harold will fire me."

"Quiet!" John yelled. "Harold won't fire you." He looked at the men. "I want every man to have a partner! I don't want anyone alone in those woods."

Jay started to speak. "Quiet!" John yelled. "Harold won't fire you!"

Mr. Jackson was in the truck. He looked at Jay. "John you got enough men," he said. "Let Jay go home! His daughters sick and he needs the work."

"Quiet!" John yelled. "Harold won't fire him!"

Mr. Andrews was in the truck. "You don't know Harold. He'll fire Jay if he's not at work! Let him go home!" he pleaded.

"Quiet!" John yelled. "I know Harold! He won't fire Jay."

Mr. Jackson looked at John. He had a suspicious look on his face. "What makes you think Harold won't fire Jay?" he asked.

John looked at Mr. Jackson. He had a snarl on his face. "First, it's Harold's truck! I got it from the mill," he said angerly.

The men looked around at the truck. It was Harold's truck. It was the one used to deliver feed.

Jay looked at John. "You took Harold's truck?" he asked.

"I needed something big enough to carry all of us," John yelled. "Second, since it's Harold's truck I figured he should drive it!"

"Harold won't fire Jay! Harold is with us!" John added.

Jay looked toward the cab. Harold was driving the truck.

Jay sat down and he laced his boots.

The truck drove quickly toward Hibdon Cemetery. As they neared, John yelled out, "I want every man to carry a lantern. I don't want to hear one word out of any of you. I don't want to see any man walking. You will run! If I see any one of you walking, I'll break your legs!"

"When we arrive, I want every man to get a partner and run toward the old section. I will search the new section. I want every man to run around the tall monuments. Look for anything unusual. If you find something, yell out! I want every man to run to whoever yells."

"If you don't see anything in the old section, run to the woods. Stay with your partner. Don't look down, look up!" John commanded.

Mr. Jackson gulped, "What do you think we will find?"

John got real serious. "I hope we find nothing," he answered.

When the truck arrived at the cemetery, Harold stopped at the gates. Every man had a lit lantern. The moon was new and it was dark. As soon as the truck stopped, the men quickly unloaded. They ran toward the old section.

John ran toward the new section. He ran to Randall's grave and he shined the lantern on it. The grave was undisturbed. He quickly ran to George's grave. He shined the lantern on it. It was undisturbed. John looked toward the old section. It was dark but he could see the lanterns moving. The men were running around the tall monuments.

He ran toward the old section. John stopped the men from searching and he split them into three groups. He pointed toward where he had found Randall. "You men go there," he ordered. "Don't look down! Look up!"

John pointed to where he had found George. "You men go there," he ordered. "Don't look down! Look up!"

The two groups ran toward the woods. "Follow me!" he ordered the third group.

John and the third group had just entered the woods when they heard a rooster crow. The dawn was one hour away but they heard a rooster crow. The men stopped. The rooster crowed again. The crow came from deep in the woods. They began to run toward the sound.

The first and second group also heard the crow. They stopped to listen. When they heard the second crow, they ran toward the sound.

The men ran quickly. They had not run far when they saw a rope tied to a tree. They looked upward to see Abram. They paused for a moment. Then, they noticed Abram was moving his legs. He was still alive!

Mr. Jackson ran to a tree. The rope was tied to a branch near the ground. He took out his pocketknife and he tried to cut it.

John ran to the tree. "Move!" he ordered.

"I'm trying to cut it!" Mr. Jackson yelled. Mr. Jackson was bent downward. He was trying to cut the rope.

John took out his gun. He walked to Mr. Jackson and he placed his boot on his back. He kicked him away from the tree. He fired his gun at the rope.

Kaboom! Kaboom!

John was holding his gun against his hip as he fired both barrels. The gun jerked in his hands. The two blasts cut the rope and shattered the limb of the tree. The tree limb was almost five inches thick. The two blasts blew the limb off the tree and shattered part of the tree. A large cloud of gun smoke came from the two blasts.

Jay was standing beside John Stepp when John fired his gun. He saw the shotgun blasts. The dimes blew half the tree away.

When the rope was blown apart, Abram fell. He was almost ten feet in the air. When he fell the men caught him. They pulled the rope off his neck. Abram was still alive. He was trying to breathe.

The men gathered around Abram. They held their lanterns toward him. The combined light was bright. Abram lay on the ground gasping for air. When John Stepp approached Abram, he knelt down. The men backed away. They looked at Abram and they looked at John Stepp. They watched Abram's face as he saw John Stepp.

Abram did not look afraid. He looked at John Stepp and he smiled. He looked at all of the men and he smiled. Then, he began choking.

"Take him to Dr. Sanders now!" John ordered. "Tell Harold to come back and get me!"

"Aren't you coming with us?" Mr. Jackson asked.

John stood and he opened the breech of his gun. The two shells ejected. He then placed two more in their place. "No! I'm staying!" John said.

The men carefully picked up Abram. Jay started to pick up the rope. "Leave it!" John commanded. Jay dropped the rope. The men took Abram to the truck and they quickly left.

John stood where Abram had fell. The men's lanterns were on the ground where they left them.

He thought he heard something and he quickly crouched. He listened for a sound, any sound. He heard nothing.

John slowly stood and he began to move quickly among the trees. He walked a large circle around where Abram fell. He walked then he stopped. He stopped to listen. He heard nothing.

He slowly worked his way through the woods. He went where he had found Randall. He saw nothing. He worked his way to where he had found George. He saw nothing. John ran to the new section. The sun was beginning to rise as he neared Randall's grave. He looked at Randall's grave. It was undisturbed.

He quickly ran to George's grave. It was undisturbed. John then ran toward the old county road. He saw nothing. He heard nothing.

The sun had risen when Harold returned. John was waiting at the gates of the cemetery. When Harold drove up, John saw his face. He knew Abram didn't make it. John got into the truck. "Take me to my car. I want to come back," John told Harold.

Neither man spoke as Harold drove to the mill. When they arrived, John got out of the truck. He walked to the driver's side. "Thank you for your help," he said.

Harold nodded. He watched John crank his car and drive off. When John had driven away, Harold broke down and cried.

The rumors about John Stepp stopped. He couldn't have killed those three boys. The men saw Abram hanging. He was still alive when they found him. He had just been strung up. It wasn't suicide either. No one could have climbed that tree and hung himself.

Everybody suddenly got religion. John Stepp came to our house everyday to ask about me. One day, Miss. Taylor was at our house when John Stepp came. Miss. Taylor didn't like John. She asked him if he was saved. She asked him if he would go to heaven when he died. John answered her question. He told her the Lord didn't want him. He had done too many bad things when he was young.

I was awake when John left. When he left, I heard Miss. Taylor curse. I had never heard her curse before. "John Stepp ain't worth a damn!" she said. "When he dies, the devils waiting for him. He's never done anything for anybody."

Several days had passed. Abram was buried in the Hibdon Cemetery and John Stepp had spent several nights watching his grave. Nothing happened. He saw or heard nothing. Abram's grave was not disturbed. John went to Abram's grave many times. He looked for signs of digging. There were none.

He went to his office one afternoon to find two letters in the mailbox. Both letters were postmarked from Memphis. John entered his office. He sat in his chair and he opened the letter from Acme Wholesale. The letter was short.

October 17, 1928

Constable Stepp,

Waiting for your arrival. I may have some information for you. Can you bring a large section of the rope with you?

R.B.
Acme Wholesale

John closed the letter. He then opened the second letter. It also was short.

October 15, 1928

John,

When are you coming? I have been looking for you. I have the medicine and I may have some information that can help.

Yours truly,

Oliver

John closed the letter. He placed it in his coat pocket and opened his desk drawer. He took a sheet of paper and wrote - Will be back - on it. He hung the paper on the door and he locked it. John walked to the diner and ordered five sandwiches. Then, he went to his car.

John Stepp Goes to Memphis

John drove his car to the Texaco filling station. As he approached, Brandon heard the rattling fender. He knew it was John Stepp. When John pulled his car beside the station, Brandon was waiting.

Brandon saluted John. "Is it time?" he asked.

John got out of his car. "Yes! How soon can you get it ready?" he asked.

"Ten minutes!" Brandon responded.

John looked at Brandon. He had a frown on his face. "Why do you salute me?" he asked.

"You're the law Mr. Stepp! If it weren't for you, those men would still be here! This is a safe town because of you! I respect the law!" Brandon answered.

John lowered his head. "Don't salute me! It makes me nervous!" John said.

Brandon stood straight and he saluted John. "Yes sir!" he said.

Brandon opened the car door and he began to remove the back seat. He looked up at John. "I hope you don't hit anything," he said. "If you hit something, it will look like the Fourth of July in Nashville."

John laughed as he walked toward the diner. When he entered, Miss. Louise was holding a large paper bag. "Going to a party?" she asked.

There were several people in the diner. When they saw John Stepp walk in, they turned their heads. When Miss. Louise asked John about a party, they quickly looked up. They wanted to see what would happen.

John had a frown on his face as he pulled money from his coat pocket. "No party! I'll be gone several days and I won't have time to stop and eat," he answered.

Miss. Louise smiled. "Where are you going?" she asked.

"Business! Official business!" John answered.

Miss. Louise stopped smiling. "I put a piece a cake in there and I made the ham sandwiches real thick," she said, as she placed the paper bag on the counter.

"Thanks!" John said. He handed Miss. Louise some money. "Keep a dime for a tip."

Mr. Benson walked around the counter. "That's OK! I heard about Abram from some of the men," he said. "The sandwiches are on me!" he added.

Mr. Benson lowered his head. "Is it about those three boys?" he asked.

John looked at Mr. Benson and Miss. Louise. He then looked at the people sitting in the diner. Everyone was looking at him. "Maybe! I'm going to Memphis to see a old friend," he answered.

Miss. Louise had a shocked look on her face. "You got friends?" she asked surprised.

"One!" John responded.

Mr. Benson looked up. "Is it Oliver?" he asked.

John was irritated by the question. "I got official business in Memphis! While I'm there, I'm going to visit an old friend. Thanks for the sandwiches and the cake but here's the money," he answered. John laid a dollar on the counter. He turned and walked out.

When the door closed, Mr. Benson looked at the people sitting in the diner. "He couldn't have killed those three boys!" he said. "Harold and Jay were there when they found Abram! If they had been there five minutes sooner, John Stepp would have saved him! Abram was hanging more than ten feet in the air. The rope was tied to a tree. Jay saw John shoot that rope with his gun. Those dimes blew half the tree apart!"

"Who killed them?" Miss. Louise asked.

"The ghost woman," Mr. Benson answered. "She killed all three of them. I don't like John Stepp but I hope he kills her! I hope he blows her all to bits with dimes."

"When did you start liking John Stepp?" one of the people in the diner asked.

Mr. Benson shrugged his shoulders. "I don't!" he answered. "It's just that someone killed those three boys and whoever did it needs to pay. Those boys never hurt anyone."

"I don't like John Stepp but I hope he kills whoever did it," he added.

When John walked to the Texaco filling station, his car was ready. Brandon had removed the back seat and placed several cans of gasoline and water in the back. He had a map lying on the hood. John walked to the hood and he looked at the map.

"They're all marked!" Brandon said as he pointed to the map. "Every Texaco filling station from Gladeville to Memphis. I marked the station near the Tennessee River but don't stop there!"

"Why not?" John asked.

Brandon pointed at the map. "It's far off the road and it will take too much time," he answered. "You got enough gas and water to take you to Jackson but stop at every station to refuel."

"Thanks!" John said.

Brandon saluted John as John got into his car. Brandon cranked it and John drove off. As he drove off, Brandon winced. He could her the fender rattling on John's car. "That would drive me crazy," Brandon remarked. He turned and walked into the station.

John had driven several miles from the Texaco filling station. He began to slow his car and then he pulled his car to the side of the road. He got out and went to the front fender. John took a wrench from his coat pocket. He looked up and down the road to make sure no one was near. Then, he bent downward and he tightened the bolts on his fender. He got back in and drove away. His car made almost no sound but the sound of the engine.

John had driven past the Tennessee River toward Memphis. He was tired. As he neared Jackson, he pulled to the side of the road and he slept. It was the sound of the two car doors closing that awakened him. A constable's car had pulled behind him and stopped. He heard a voice.

"Is anything wrong?" a man's voice asked.

"Get out of the car!" another man, yelled.

John raised up. It was dark and the headlamps of the constable's car were shining on his car. He slowly got out.

The two constables watched John slowly emerge from his car. When John stood before them, they were amazed at how tall he was. "I'm on official business," John said. "I'm a constable."

The two constables laughed. "Not from around here!" one of them said.

Both constables were wearing gun holsters. "Raise your hands!" one of the constables, said, as he moved his hand toward his gun.

"I wouldn't do that! I'm a constable!" John ordered.

The two men stopped. They looked at each other then they looked at John. One of them asked, "If you are a constable, where are you from?" As he was speaking, he started to reach for his gun.

"I warned you not to do that!" John commanded. "I'm from Gladeville!"

The constable stopped reaching toward his gun. The two men looked at each other and they began to laugh.

"What's funny!" John asked.

The two constables laughed. "You got nerve!" one of them said.

The two constables laughed. "You don't have nerve, your crazy!" the other one said.

The two constables laughed. "Gladeville's only got one constable, John Stepp," one of the two said. "John Stepp's killed fifty men. He'll kill you for impersonating him."

The two constables laughed. Then, they stopped laughing. "Put up your hands," one of them ordered as he began to reach for his gun.

"I warned you not to do that!" John commanded. "If you put your hand on that gun, it'll be fifty-two."

The two constables stopped and they looked at each other. "Can you prove your John Stepp?" one of the constables asked.

"What do you want to see, my badge?" John asked.

"The gun! I want to see the gun!" one of the two constables, replied.

John reached into his coat pocket and pulled out his gun.

The two constables froze. They looked at John and they looked at his gun. "It's him! It's really him!" one of the constables said to the other.

John replaced his gun and he took out his badge. He held his badge toward them and he began to walk toward the two constables. As he walked toward them, they walked backward.

"I'm on business!" John said. "I'm on official business! I'm going to Memphis and I stopped to rest. I'll be moving on!"

The two constables stopped. "Yes sir!" they both said.

John replaced his badge and he turned toward his car. He began to walk toward his car when one of the constables' spoke, "How many men have you killed?" he asked.

John stopped and he turned. "I don't rightly know! It's more than fifty," he answered.

The two constables looked at each. "More than fifty!" one of them said.

John turned and he began to walk toward his car. One of the constables spoke. "Mr. Stepp! Would you have really killed us?" he gulped.

John turned. "If you had put your hand on that gun, I would have killed both of you! I don't know if your constables or not! A real constable would not have let me get as close to you as I did," he answered.

"The car looks official and only constables carry Colts. No, I wouldn't have killed you," he said. "I would have blown your legs off!"

The two constables looked at each other and they gulped. They watched John crank his car. He got in and drove off.

When John's car was far down the road, the two constables looked at each other. Their noses curled upward. "I shit my pants!" one of them said.

"So did I!" the other said. "Do you think anybody will believe us?" he added.

"No!" the constable said. "Nobody will believe we told John Stepp to raise his hands and we lived to tell about it!"

Acme Wholesale

The Acme Wholesale Company was just opening when John drove up. He took a box from the back seat area and he walked into the door. A young man greeted him.

"May I speak to R.B.?" John asked. "My name is John Stepp."

"He's waiting for you," the man replied. He pointed toward an opened door. "I'll get Jacob."

John walked into a small office. He sat down when an elderly man walked in. The elderly man smiled. "My name is Jacob. R.B. is coming," he said.

A few minutes passed before a tall man entered the office. He closed the door. "Constable Stepp," he said. He leaned forward and shook John's hand. "I asked Jacob to sit in because he has some questions." John nodded his head.

"Can I see it!" Jacob asked. John handed Jacob the box. Jacob opened it and he took the rope out. He looked at it and smiled. Then he took a knife from his pocket. "Can I cut it?" Jacob asked. John nodded his head.

Jacob tried to cut the rope with his knife but it wouldn't cut. He took a straight razor from his pocket. He cut a small piece and he twirled it in his hands. "Just what I thought," he said.

Jacob looked at R.B. "I'm certain!" he said.

"Thanks," R.B. replied. "You can go now!"

Jacob handed the rope to John. "Can I have a length of it?" he asked. "Not a long piece. Maybe four feet?"

"Take twelve feet if you like," John responded.

Jacob's face lit up. He measured twelve feet and he cut it. He coiled it up and nodded his head to John. "Thank you!" he said.

R.B. opened the door and Jacob left. As Jacob left, he had a big smile on his face. He held the coiled rope like it was a great treasure. R.B. closed the door after Jacob left.

R.B. sat down in front of John. "Jacob has been with us many years. He was here when we started and he handles all of our rope. When I showed him the sample you sent us, he couldn't sleep," he said.

"You have made him a very happy man," R.B. added.

"Did you sell it?" John asked.

R.B. frowned. "I thought you would like to know about the rope before I answered that question," he said.

"Is it important?" John asked.

"Yes!" R.B. answered.

"Where did it come from?" John asked.

R.B. stood and he picked up the coiled rope. "Jacob knows his rope," he said. "That may not be important to you or me but it is to him. He likes to make sure that we sell quality products. We sell a lot of rope. It comes up the river from New Orleans and down the river from St. Louis. Jacob arranges every purchase and he grades the quality."

"Last year, we got a piece that come from Montana. This piece was very high in quality. Jacob made a lariat out of it. He sent it to Tom Mix."

"Tom Mix?" John asked.

R.B. laughed, "He sent it Tom Mix and Tom sent him a letter and a autographed picture. In the picture, Tom is twirling the lariat."

R.B. sat down. "Jacob has the letter and the autographed picture. He keeps it at the bank in the safe. I think he stops at the bank once a week to look at the picture and read the letter," he said.

"What does Tom Mix have to do with this rope?" John asked.

"Nothing, but perhaps everything," R.B. said.

"This is the same type of rope that Jacob made Tom Mix's lariat out of?" John asked.

"No," R.B. answered.

John was confused. He did not know what R.B. was talking about. "You said this was important?" John asked.

"It is!" R.B. answered.

"What does Tom Mix have to do with this rope?" John asked.

R.B. took a deep breath. "There are several young men that joke with Jacob. They had seen the Tom Mix letter and picture. There was a rodeo that came into town several months ago. The men told Jacob that Tom Mix was going to be there. Jacob believed them," he laughed. "He got his picture and letter from the bank and he went to the rodeo. He expected to see Tom Mix twirling his lariat."

"Tom Mix wasn't there. There were different cowboys and Indians. There was a stagecoach robbery and sharpshooters," he added.

John was irritated. "What does all of this have to do with the rope?" he asked.

R.B. leaned close toward John. "There were Arabian horses. They came all the way from Arabia. The horses were all decked out in fancy saddles. They were alleged to have been the property of some king," he said.

"Jacob saw the Arabian horses and he saw how they were made up. The bridles were made of leather and an unusual rope."

R.B. leaned back in his chair. "The sample of the rope you sent us is the same as the rope used on the bridles of the Arabian horses. The rope was made in Arabia. It was not made in the United States," he added.

John was puzzled.

"The rope used in the bridles of the Arabian horses was made special. Hemp has a short growth cycle. Most rope made in the United States is made of short strands. These ropes had strands as long as four feet. The hemp had been grown for many years and the rope was hand made. The rope was made for a special purpose! The rope used on the bridles of those Arabian horse was made for a king! The rope sample you sent us is the same," R.B. said.

"What are you saying?" John asked.

R.B stood up. "If Jacob had not went to the rodeo, he never would have seen those Arabian horses. The rope was made in Arabia! It did not come from the United States. The rope was made special! We didn't sell it! We have never seen it!" R.B. said.

John was puzzled. "How did rope made in Arabia come to Gladeville," he asked.

"That's the question Jacob had," R.B. said. "Where did you get it? We want to sell it! How much do you have?" R.B. asked.

John lowered his head. "I found it in the woods. It was tied to a tree. I have three pieces. They are all the same length," he said.

"How long are they?" R.B. asked.

"They are all the same the same length," John said. He looked upward at R.B. "They are all eighty feet."

"Eighty feet!" R.B. yelled. "Name your price! Any price!"

"I can't sell them! They are evidence in a case I'm working on," John answered.

"You're a constable!" R.B. said. "Name your price!"

John stood and he glared at R.B. "They're not for sale! I wanted to know if you sold it! I didn't come here to sell it!"

R.B smiled. "I understand! Let me know when the case is over! Come back to Memphis! I will make it worth your time," he said.

John glared at R.B. "I can't sell it! What is so special about this rope? What makes it so special?" John asked.

§

R.B. laughed, "It's the strands! They're long and thick! You can't cut it unless the knife is razor sharp! You can't break it!"

"I did!" John said.

"With what?" R.B. laughed.

John reached into his coat and he pulled out his gun. "A young boy was hanging from the end of one of those ropes. I cut it with my gun!" he said.

R.B. laughed. "A shotgun won't cut it!" he said.

"This one did!" John answered.

R.B. laughed. "What do you shoot out of that gun, dimes?" he asked.

"Yes!" John responded.

R.B.'s face went blank. He looked at John Stepp and he looked at his gun. "Dimes? You shoot dimes from that gun? Are you the constable in Gladeville?" he asked.

"Yes!" John answered.

R.B.'s face was solemn. "I didn't know who you were! I didn't mean to imply anything!" he said. R.B. was real nervous. He looked at the closed door. "Mr. Stepp! I didn't realize who you were! Please forgive me!"

"What is special about this rope?" John asked.

R.B. gulped. "It was made for a special purpose! It was made for a king! It wasn't made here! We have never sold it! We have never seen it!" he answered. "I want to buy all you have! We can sell it to someone important!"

"Like who?" John asked. "Tom Mix?"

R.B. lowered his head. "We were hoping we could get some more of that rope. I planned to have a special saddle and bridle made with that rope and present it to Tom Mix myself," he said. "My picture would be in all of the newspapers. I may get a part in one of his movies."

John Stepp shrugged his shoulders. "I don't know much about Tom Mix but I don't think he wants a rope that was made to hang someone," he said gruffly. "If he knew where I got it, I don't think he would want it. I don't think he would want it on his horse."

John Stepp opened the door. He walked out and he stopped at the front desk. "I'm looking for a Catholic Church. I think it may be near. Can you point me in the right direction," he asked.

"It's near the river by the bridge. You can't miss it," the man replied.

The Blessing

John drove up to the St. Luke's Rectory. When he stopped his car, Father Oliver came running out to greet him.

Father Oliver had a big grin on his face. "John it has been a long time!" he shouted.

John got out of his car. He too had a big grin on his face. "Oliver!" he said.

They stood looking at each other. Both men had a big grin on their faces. Then, they embraced. When they hugged each other, Father Oliver felt John's gun through his coat. Father Oliver moved backward.

"You still carry that thing!" Father Oliver said.

John looked at his coat and he placed his hand over the gun. "Yes!" he replied. "I never go anywhere without it."

"Let me see it?" Father Oliver asked.

John reached into his coat and he pulled his gun out. It was a double-barrel sawed-off shotgun. "Sure," he said as he handed it to Father Oliver. "You can shoot it if you want."

Father Oliver took John's gun. He held it in his hands and he pointed it downward. "No, I had better not but I sure would like to," he said.

A funny look came over Father Oliver's face as he held John's gun. It was a sad look. Father Oliver held the gun and he opened the breech. It was loaded. There were two shells He pulled one of the two shells out and he looked at the end. The shell had been opened and re-closed. "Dimes?" Father Oliver asked.

John answered, "Yes!"

Father Oliver replaced the shell and he held the gun upward. He looked down the barrels. "I think about this gun a lot," he said. "I think about this gun and that night."

"I don't!" John said.

Father Oliver had a frown on his face. He looked down the barrels. "I think about this gun and the look on David's face when those dimes struck him," he said.

"I don't think about that either," John replied.

Father Oliver lowered the gun and he looked at John. Oliver had a disappointed look on his face.

John had an angry look on his face. "It was self-defense Oliver!" he said. "It was us or them!"

Father Oliver handed the gun to John. "I know! I know! If it wasn't for this gun, I wouldn't be here today!" he said.

"You did OK!" John said.

"I don't mean that! If it wasn't for this gun I wouldn't have become a priest," Father Oliver said.

John replaced his gun in his coat. "You always had religion! It was a matter of time! I saw it in the way you acted! This gun had nothing to do with it!" John said.

Father Oliver lowered his head. "Yes it did! When I saw David lying there blown all to pieces I knew one day that would happen to me. I didn't want to go like that! You need to think about that John," he said. "You need to think about things."

"I think about a lot of things! That is not one of them," John replied.

Father Oliver raised his head and laughed. He placed his hand on John's shoulder. "You haven't changed!" he said.

John laughed, "I'm older and uglier." He looked at Father Oliver. "You got fat!"

Father Oliver laughed. "What ever happened to them?" he asked.

John had a stern look on his face. "They're gone! They're all gone!" he said.

Father Oliver placed his hand on his chin. "It seemed they would never go away. Is Knuckles gone too?" he asked.

"They're all gone!" John replied.

"Where did they go?" Father Oliver asked.

"It doesn't matter! The important thing is they are gone," John answered.

Father Oliver laughed and he placed both hands on John's shoulders. "It is so good to see you!" he said. "You are a constable in Gladeville. What is it like?" he asked.

"Gladeville is a nice town. There are real good folks there!" John replied.

"Any trouble?" Father Oliver asked.

John looked away from Father Oliver toward the street. He looked to see if anyone was near. "Not anymore!" he said. "Gladeville is a nice town. I plan on keeping it that way!"

Father Oliver looked at John's face. "Were we that wild?" Father Oliver asked. "Were we that tough?"

"Tough enough to survive. I'm sure the Lord didn't take all of the mean out of you," John answered.

Father Oliver looked at John. He removed his hands from his shoulders then he placed one hand on John's shoulder. "The Lord has done a lot of things for me. The Lord will do a lot of things for you if you will let him. I would like to tell you about the Lord," he said.

"Oliver, there is no one more I trust and respect. I would like to listen to what you have to say but I am in a hurry! One day I'll come back and listen to what you have to tell me. I know you speak from the heart. Who knows, maybe I'll become a priest like you. Right now, I have to get back to Gladeville," John said.

Father Oliver grined and he laughed. "Follow me! Everything is ready!" Father Oliver said.

Father Oliver walked to the church and John followed. They entered the door and walked near the altar and Father Oliver knelled. Then, John followed him into a small chapel. There was a candle and an opened Bible lying on a small table. On the table was a brass bowl filled with water.

Father Oliver went to a chair and he picked up a robe. He placed the robe over his head and pulled it on. Then, he lit the candle. When the candle was lit, he turned to John. "Sit," he said.

John sat in a chair near the table. Father Oliver stood near the altar. He began to speak. "The Church don't believe in ghosts. There is the Holy Ghost but that isn't a ghost like that woman people claim to have seen. The Church believes in Saints. Saints are people who did God's will. I figure if there are Saints on the side of God there must be something similar on the devil's side."

"When I received your letter, I asked around. The Bible doesn't say anything about a woman ghost." Father Oliver looked at John. "Not a real ghost. The Bible talks of spirits."

"Oliver, I don't believe in ghosts or spirits! This woman is real! I don't know what she is up to but she ain't no spirit or ghost," John said.

Father Oliver laughed, "When I go into a fight, I win!"

John laughed. "You remember that?" John asked.

Father Oliver stopped laughing. "I remember everything!" he said.

John was irritated. "I'm really in a hurry, Oliver," he said. "Just give me the medicine and I will go! I finished my business but I need to get back."

Father Oliver walked to the opened Bible and he turned the pages. "It won't take long," he said.

John stood. "What are you talking about? Are you going to baptize me?" John asked.

Father Oliver looked up from the Bible. "No!" he said. He looked at John. "When I began studying to be a priest, I read a lot and I talked to many educated men. There are a lot of things in the Bible that I believe in. I believe in good and evil. I believe in God and the devil. I believe anything is possible. It is possible that the woman is a ghost."

He walked to a cabinet and he took out a brass ball with a handle on it. He took out a small bottle of oil and he placed it on the table. "I usually use this for baptisms but it should work," he said.

"Work for what?" John said.

"The blessing!" Father Oliver replied. "If that woman is real, those dimes will tear her all to pieces. If that woman is a ghost, they may not hurt her at all. If that woman is a real ghost, only God can help you!"

"What are going to bless?" John asked.

Father Oliver went to the small cabinet and he took out a bag. The bag rattled when he picked it up. He placed the bag on the table. "Hand me your gun," he asked.

"What for?" John asked.

"I'm going to bless these dimes and your gun. I'm going to sprinkle them with Holy water," Father Oliver answered.

John let out a big laugh. He stood and he laughed, "Oliver, If I didn't know you I would think you were pranking me."

Father Oliver looked real serious at John. "We have known each other for a long time. I trust you with my life. I'm a priest and I have taken a vow against violence," he said. "I don't know what you are up against. You are not sure yourself. You would not have written me unless you thought I could somehow help. If I had not taken my vow, I would be with you. I would stand beside you."

John was angry. "I didn't write you to come help me fight!" he said.

Father Oliver was angry. He moved around the table and stood in front of John. "Why did you write me?" he asked.

John slowly turned his head. "I was coming to Memphis on business. It has been a long time. I just wanted to see you. I wanted to see how you were. I thought you might know someone who had some real medicine for a young girl that is sick. Dr. Sanders is old. I don't think he knows the new medicine," he said.

"Dr. Sanders?" Father Oliver asked. "He's still alive?"

"Yes! He has been treating a young girl for sometime. I don't think he's any good," John responded.

Father Oliver laughed, "Good enough for this!" He raised his right pants leg. There was a large scar on the calf of his right leg. "He fixed me up real good!"

Father Oliver got a real sad look his face. He lowered his head. "There wasn't anything he could do for David!" he said, under his breath. "There wasn't anything left to fix!" Father Oliver lowered his pants leg. He looked up at John. "There wasn't enough left of those six men to fill a fruit jar."

John looked at Father Oliver. "That was a long time ago! He's old now! I don't think he knows as much as he could," John said.

"That's not it!" Father Oliver yelled. "If you wanted medicine you could get it in Nashville! You didn't have to drive all the way to Memphis for it!"

"I have known you a long time. We went through a lot together. Why did you write me?" Father Oliver asked again.

John looked at Father Oliver. "A lot of strange things have happened that don't make sense. Those boys died by being hung and there is talk of a ghost woman. I don't believe in ghosts! I knew you were a priest. I knew if I asked you about ghosts, you wouldn't laugh," he answered. "I knew if it was true, you might know how to fight her."

"That's what I thought," Father Oliver said. "John Stepp don't need no help in fighting. If anyone but you had written me that letter I would have laughed. I knew there was something more than a simple suicide. I don't believe in ghosts either but if it is a ghost, you will need something more than dimes to kill it! You will need dimes blessed and sprinkled with Holy water."

"This is no suicide! Someone murdered those two boys."

John interrupted Oliver, "Three! There are three dead boys."

Father Oliver was surprised. "Three dead boys! Did the third one die from hanging?" he asked.

"All three of them died the same way. They all died from hanging. Someone tried to dig two of them up. The last boy said the three of them had seen the ghost woman. He said they tried to catch her," John said. "I don't believe in ghosts but I saw something strange on Randall and George's grave. Whoever tried to dig them up didn't use a shovel. They used their hands. I could see an imprint of hands in the dirt. The hands were small."

"They were made by a woman!"

Father Oliver was shocked. He sat down in a chair.

"Did anybody else see her or come close to her?" Father Oliver asked.

John remarked, "Mr. Lewis saw her. He said she was trying to get to his son's grave and a rooster stopped her. Sarah Jane said she came real close to her and she tried to grab her foot. The rooster tried to spur the ghost woman. Several people saw her when they were on a hayride."

Father Oliver looked up at John. "What kind of rooster?" he asked.

John laughed, "A rooster no one sees during the daytime. The rooster only comes at night. He's Sarah Jane's pet. The rooster comes to her house and walks back and forth on the porch."

Father Oliver looked downward. "This girl named Sarah Jane, is she the girl you asked me to get medicine for?" he asked.

"Yes!" John responded. "She will get sick, then she will get better. Every time I have seen her, she was sick."

"You had better leave," Father Oliver said. "You're needed in Gladeville." He stood and he went to the small cabinet. He removed several matchboxes and a bottle and he placed them on the table. "There are instructions in one of the matchboxes. The pills need to be crushed and mixed with whiskey," he said.

"This isn't whiskey, it's scotch. It will work just as well," he added.

Father Oliver sat down in a chair.

"How much do I owe you for the medicine?" John asked, as he reached into his pants pocket.

Father Oliver waved his hand in the air. "Nothing!" he said. "One of the members is a doctor. I married him and I baptized his son. He gave it to me when I asked."

John looked at the bottle. "This is not moonshine! It's high test! It looks expensive! Where did you get it?" John asked.

Father Oliver waved his hand in the air. "Sometimes people do bad things and they ask for forgiveness. It is expensive! The scotch came from Scotland. The man who gave it to me had a lot of things on his mind. It was a small price for God's forgiveness! It was free!" Father Oliver replied.

John picked up the matchboxes and the bottle. He placed them inside his coat. He looked at Father Oliver. Father Oliver just sat in the chair and he had a sad look on his face. "It has been good seeing you again," John said. Father Oliver did not answer.

John walked to the door when he stopped. He turned and looked at Father Oliver. Father Oliver just sat in the chair. He had a sad look on his face.

"We were pretty wild when we were young and we did a lot of things I'm not proud of," John said. "One thing we always did was being honest with each other. I was real happy when I heard you got religion. Somehow, I felt you were safe. You were like a brother to me."

"You did answer my question about ghosts. You're probably right! If she is a ghost, my dimes won't hurt her. I need all the help I can get in this fight! If you really believe this blessing will help, lets do it!" John said.

"When I go into a fight, I win!" he added.

Father Oliver smiled. He stood and he went to the table. He opened the bag and poured the dimes onto the table. John handed Father Oliver his gun. Then, he sat down.

"Where did you get all those dimes?" John asked.

"I have been saving them from the collection plate since I got your letter," Father Oliver replied. "I thought you might need them."

John raised his eyebrows; "You robbed the church?"

Father Oliver laughed, "I didn't rob the Church! If your going to fight a ghost or an evil spirit, I don't think a few dimes will hurt the Church. It is for a good cause."

"If it is a real ghost, why here? Why Gladeville?" John asked.

Father Oliver was looking at the dimes. He looked upward at John and smiled. "It's a long story and it includes me," he answered.

"I got time!" John replied.

Father Oliver smiled and he walked to a chair beside John and he sat down. "I was scared that night! Real scared!" he said. "I just left! I just walked away. It seemed like years but it was only days when I realized I was in St. Louis."

"I was standing in front of a seminary. It was late and I just went in. There were several priests there. One of the priests was Father Andrew. I told them I wanted to become a priest and they asked me why."

"I told them! Then, they asked me to wait outside. I waited for about ten minutes and Father Andrew came to get me. They accepted me!"

"Just like that?" John asked.

Father Oliver laughed, "No! Not just like that!"

"It would be years later before I discovered the real reason they accepted me. It was Father Andrew. Father Andrew helped me. He helped with my studies. Sometimes we would sit and talk for hours."

"When I was ordained, Father Andrew wanted to see me. I went to his room and he told me." Father Oliver lowered his head. He looked at John. "He told me everything!"

John was puzzled. "What did he tell you?" he asked.

Father Oliver stood. "They didn't want me! None of the priests wanted me! I wasn't Catholic. They thought I was running from the law. They thought I was a criminal!" he said.

John laughed, "They were right!"

Father Oliver laughed and he sat down. "It was Father Andrew that convinced them!" he said. "Father Andrew told them that the Lord sent me to them. He told them that one day I would do something great! He told them that the Lord could change anyone. He convinced them to take me."

"Father Andrew believed that he had been chosen to do something great. He believed I was that something. He believed that he was chosen to be there at that place and time. He believed he was there to convince the others to accept me."

"I asked Father Andrew, Why Me? Father Andrew said, Why not!"

"The Lord does not see cities or towns. The Lord does not see states or countries. The Lord sees everything. Why not me! I was a sinner and a man. I was no different from any other."

"The Lord had chosen me for something great. What it was he did not know."

John looked at Father Oliver. "Why not Gladeville?" he said.

Father Oliver stood quickly. "Why not Gladeville?" he said. "The Lord knows no boundaries. The devil knows no boundaries. Why not Gladeville?"

"I think I was destined to do this! I think the blessing is needed! Father Andrew would do it if he was here!" Father Oliver added.

"Where is he?" John asked. "I would like to meet him."

Father Oliver walked to the table. "He's dead! He died several months ago," he said. Father Oliver lowered his head. Then, he smiled. "He would have liked to meet you!" Father Oliver grinned. "He knew all about you and me. Most of what we talked about was you and me and the things we did."

"Did you tell him everything?" John asked.

Father Oliver laughed, "Only the good parts! Most of it was boring."

"I really liked him!" Father Oliver said. "He never talked about himself until the final days he was sick. I would visit him when I could and he would talk about himself. He was so proud of me."

Father Oliver laughed. "I think he told me things about himself he never told anyone else. Like his name," he chuckled.

"What about his name?" John asked.

Father Oliver laughed. "He hated his name. Father Andrew's family was Catholic. There were five boys. Father Andrew was the youngest. Each of the boys was named after an apostle. There was Mark, Luke, John, and Peter. Father Andrew was the youngest. He was named Andrew," he laughed.

"Father Andrew said when he born, the good names were taken. He was stuck with Andrew. He didn't like the name so people called him Andy," he added.

Father Oliver laughed. "I was with him when he died. I gave him the last rites and he asked me to use the name Andy not Andrew. He wanted to make sure the Lord knew who he was," Father Oliver laughed.

John paused. He looked carefully at Father Oliver. "Just exactly when did he die?" he asked.

Father Oliver looked at John. "It was about the time you found the first boy," he answered. "When did you find the first boy?"

"I found him Thursday August 2," John answered.

Father Oliver looked up at John and he sighed, "Father Andrew died Monday July 30."

"Did Father Andrew believe in ghosts?" John asked.

Father Oliver looked at the dimes and he scattered them on the table. "Oh Yes!" he answered. "He believed it was possible. He believed everything in the Bible. He believed anything was possible."

Father Oliver looked at John. "He taught me everything I know. I believed him! He once told me that you were chosen for a great task! Perhaps that is why we are here!"

John laughed, "The Lord don't want me! I've done too many bad things!"

Father Oliver had a serious look on his face. "Father Andrew taught me that a man can do a lot of bad things and one good deed can wipe the slate clean," he said. "I have seen it! I have seen bad men turn good and good men turn bad. I suspect when you die, the pearly gates will be opened not closed."

Father Oliver made the sign of the cross over John's gun and the dimes. "Supplices ergo te, Domine, deprecamur," he chanted.

"What did you say?" John asked.

"It's Latin. The Mass is done in Latin. I have never blessed anything like this so I am using the blessing of the sacrament," he replied.

"Speak in English," John said. "I want to know what you're saying."

Father Oliver nodded. He made the sign of the cross over the dimes and John's gun. He chanted, "And so, Father, we bring you these gifts. We ask you to make them Holy by the power of your Spirit."

"My coat and hat," John laughed. "I always wear them. If the dimes don't kill her, I might have to fight her with my bare hands." He began to take off his coat and his hat.

Father Oliver smiled. John placed his coat and hat on the table and Father Oliver made the sign of the cross again. Then he chanted. He sprinkled the dimes and the gun with Holy water. Then he sprinkled John's coat and hat.

"Better get me while you're at it!" John said. He knelled beside the table and lowered his head.

Father Oliver walked to John. He placed oil on his finger and he made the sign of the cross on John's forehead with the oil. Then, he placed his hand on John's head.

"Bless this man who seeks to do good. Bless this man who seeks to protect others. Bless this man as he seeks to battle evil. Protect this man from evil," Father Oliver said.

He made the sign of the cross and he sprinkled John with the Holy water. Then he chanted, "In the name of the Father, and the Son, and the Holy Ghost."

John stood and he put on his coat and hat. He placed his gun in the large pocket of his coat and he placed the bag of dimes in the right pocket of his coat. "If the woman is really a ghost, you will need to get real close to her," Father Oliver said.

"How close?" John asked.

Father Oliver walked to John and he placed his hand on John's shoulder.

"Oliver, I don't plan on getting that close to anybody I'm fighting," John said.

"Get as close as you can and shoot her in the face. Those blessed dimes may hurt her if you shoot her in the face," Father Oliver said.

John laughed. "Do you really believe that woman is a ghost?" he asked.

Father Oliver laughed. "It doesn't matter what I believe. It is what the people of Gladeville believe that is important. If they think she is ghost, give them a ghost," he said.

"What if she isn't a ghost? The last boy found dead was Abram. He said she was a crazy woman. What if she is a crazy woman like Abram said?" John asked.

"It will take a broom to sweep her up!" Father Oliver laughed.

John and Father Oliver walked to John's car. John got in and Father Oliver cranked the engine. He walked to the driver's side. "It's really good seeing you. I sometimes worried about you. We have always been honest with each other. I heard that Knuckles and the others just disappeared. Did you have anything to do with them disappearing?" Father Oliver asked. "You can tell me! I'm a priest! Any confession will be held."

"It was nice seeing you too," John said. "I never worried about you because you could take care of yourself. Your mother and father were proud of you when you became a priest. I'm proud of you! It's late and I need to get back to Gladeville."

John chuckled, " I got a ghost woman to fight and I'll need all my strength."

Father Oliver had a disappointed look on his face. He placed his hand on John's shoulder. "I don't know if that woman is a ghost or not. If she is a real ghost, those blessed dimes might hurt her," he said.

John turned the engine off and he sat for a minute. "If this woman is a real ghost, where does the rooster come in? What does the rooster have to do with all of this?" John asked. "The rooster fought the ghost woman twice. She seems to be afraid of him."

Father Oliver shrugged his shoulders. "I don't know. The ghost may have come back to take the soul of an innocent. Perhaps the rooster is somehow trying to stop this," he answered.

John laughed, "Those three boys weren't innocent."

Father Oliver frowned. He looked away from John and he said, "In a way, we were innocent. Those three boys may not be innocent in your eyes but they may be innocent in God's eye."

Father Oliver walked to the front of John's car and he cranked it. John pulled up real slow and he looked at Father Oliver. "Oliver, about your question. It was self-defense," John said. He patted his coat where his gun was.

Father Oliver looked at John. Slowly a smile came on his face. "The more I talk to you the more I remember," he said. Father Oliver smiled. "It was six of them against the two of us. David had a pistol and you were holding that sawed-off shotgun. They thought you were out of range. They didn't know and I didn't know that those shells were loaded with dimes." Father Oliver paused. "I'll never forget the look on David's face when he laughed and held his pistol up. I'll never forget the look on his face when those dimes struck him."

Father Oliver turned his head away from John. "How many shots did you fire?" he asked.

"I don't remember," John said.

"They didn't have a chance!" Father Oliver said. He looked at John. "They didn't have a chance," he repeated.

"To answer your second question, I fired both barrels three times," John said.

Father Oliver laughed, "I thought you didn't remember."

"I'm getting old, Oliver! My memory comes and goes," John laughed.

"Did I help you?" Father Oliver asked.

"Yes!" John said. "More than you will ever know!"

John sped quickly away. He drove toward Nashville.

Strange Happenings

It was near sundown and Mr. Jackson and his wife sat at the eating table. I was very ill. My mother would come into my room and look at me. My fever had dropped but I didn't feel well. My chest and my head hurt. My mother checked on me and she returned to the eating table.

"Joe saw her last night!" Mr. Jackson said. "Do you think she will come tonight?" he asked.

My father looked at Mr. Jackson. "Yes! When the sun sets she will be here. Andy will be here too!" he said.

"Where is the rooster?" Mr. Jackson's wife Sandra asked.

My mother spoke up; "He comes to the gate. He walks back and forth by the gate."

J.B. was standing by the door. The door was opened and he was watching the sun. He could see the sunlight fading. It came over the back of our house and lit up the woods near our gate. When the sun dropped, J.B. called out; "She's here!"

Mr. and Mrs. Jackson slowly stood. They walked to the opened door and they looked out. At the edge of the woods, near our gate, a woman was standing.

They could see her because of her white dress. The dress was long and it touched the ground. The dress showed up white against the dark woods. The woman was young, about nineteen. She had long, dark hair. The woman just stood. She looked toward the gate.

Mr. and Mrs. Jackson looked toward the gate. A large, white rooster was walking back and forth. The rooster walked the distance of the gate and then stopped. The rooster looked toward the woman and crouched. Then, he began to walk again.

Mrs. Jackson was unnerved. "Who is she?" she asked.

"I don't know!" my mother replied. "I think she is the woman that dances in the graveyard."

Mr. Jackson gulped. "She's dead?" he asked.

"I don't know," my father replied. "When the sun comes up, Andy crows. Then, she's gone."

Mrs. Jackson folded her arms. "Humph!" she said. "If that woman is bothering folks, John Stepp needs to arrest her!"

"I didn't know you liked John Stepp?" my mother asked.

"I don't!" Mrs. Jackson replied. "He's our constable! It's his job to arrest her!"

"She hasn't done anything but stand there," my father said.

"No!" Mr. Jackson said. "She's waiting for Sarah Jane to die! When Sarah Jane dies, she will come into this house and take her spirit!"

Mrs. Jackson shrugged her shoulders. "Not if John Stepp is here! He'll kill her!" she said.

"Nobody knows where John is," Mr. Jackson replied. "Nobody has seen him in two days."

"The double moon is coming," Mrs. Jackson said. "She's waiting for the double moon! Someone had better get John Stepp!"

"I went to his office twice," my father said. "He's not there!"

"He'll come!" Mrs. Jackson said. "That's the kind of trouble he takes care of! He ain't worth a damn! When you need him you can't find him but when something like this happens, he always shows!"

"Sounds like you like John Stepp," my father said.

"No!" Mrs. Jackson said. "He ain't worth a damn! He's never done anything for anybody! If that ghost woman tries to hurt Sarah Jane, John Stepp will blow her to hell with that gun of his!"

Mr. and Mrs. Jackson looked outward toward the woods. They looked at the woman standing by the trees and then they looked at the gate. The rooster was walking back and forth in front of the gate.

Mr. Jackson looked to his wife. "Let's go!" he said.

Mrs. Jackson looked at the woods and she looked at the gate. "You had better get John Stepp! He'll kill her if she tries to hurt Sarah Jane!" she said.

My father and mother looked at Mr. and Mrs. Jackson.

"John Stepp took care of those men! He'll take care of her!" Mrs. Jackson snarled.

John drove straight to Gladeville. He stopped for gasoline and water. He did not stop to eat or sleep. He was several miles from Gladeville when he stopped his car. He pulled to the side of the road and he got out. He looked to see if anyone was near. Then, he took a wrench from his coat pocket. He bent downward near the fender and he loosened several bolts. He got into his car and drove to Gladeville. As he drove, the fender rattled.

Brandon heard the rattling fender. He was waiting for John when the car drove up. "How was the trip?" Brandon asked.

John stopped the engine and stepped out. He stretched and yawned. "Long and tiring," he answered.

"Any trouble on the road?" Brandon asked.

John looked at Brandon. He had a frown on his face. "No!" he answered.

"Fix my backseat. Don't touch that box!" he ordered.

Brandon saluted John. "Yes sir! I got news!" he said.

"What news?" John asked.

"Lots of things! No one has died but everyone is talking about the ghost woman," he said.

John looked at Brandon carefully. "What about her?" he asked.

Brandon walked close to John. He looked around to see if anyone was near. "A lot of people have seen her. She comes to the woods by Jay's house. Sarah Jane is real sick and people think she is waiting for Sarah Jane to die," he whispered.

"Is that all?" John asked.

Brandon whispered, "Everyone thinks she killed those three boys. They don't think you did it!"

John laughed, "That's news!"

Brandon whispered, "Tonight is the double moon! People think Sarah Jane will die tonight and the ghost woman will take her spirit."

John frowned. "I don't believe in ghosts but if a woman is scaring the folks I will put a stop to it!" he said.

Brandon looked at John. "What are you going to do?" he asked.

John smiled. "I'll visit Jay tonight. I want to see this woman who people think is a ghost," he said.

"She comes after the sun sets," Brandon said. "She stands by the edge of the woods looking at the house. She won't come near the gate."

John had a puzzled look on his face. "Why won't she come near the gate? If she is a ghost she can't get Sarah Jane's spirit from the woods," he said.

"It's the rooster!" Brandon whispered.

"What rooster?" John asked.

Brandon leaned real close to John. "It's the rooster that stopped her from getting to Randall's grave. Mr. Wilson saw the rooster! The rooster guards the gate. He won't let her come near," he whispered.

John looked at Brandon. "How many ghosts are there?" he asked.

Brandon looked puzzled by John's question. "Only one!" Brandon replied.

John laughed. He looked at Brandon. "Thanks for your help. If there is anything I can do for you," John said.

Brandon smiled. "You already did! If it wasn't for you and Oliver I would be dead," he answered.

John turned and he walked to his office. He checked the mailbox. There were no letters. He went inside and lay on his bed. He was tired. He didn't take off his hat or coat. He fell asleep quickly.

It was three o'clock when someone knocked on his door. John rose quickly. It was almost instinct that he pulled his gun. As he stood, he cocked both barrels. John looked to the window. Jay Singer was standing outside. He returned his gun to his coat pocket.

John motioned for Jay to come in.

Jay walked in. "John I need your help!" he said.

"Is it the woman that's been bothering you?" John asked.

"Yes! Sarah Jane is real sick. The woman comes at night and stands by the woods. She hasn't done anything but she is scaring us. She is scaring Sarah Jane," Jay replied.

"Have you talked to her? Have you asked her who she is?" John asked.

Jay lowered his head. "No. I have not gone near her," he said. "She comes at sun set and just stands looking. When the sun rises, she leaves. I don't know where she goes. I am afraid to follow her."

"I'll come tonight and talk to her. I'll get her to leave and quit bothering you folks," John said. He reached into his coat pocket and he pulled out several matchboxes. He reached into his other pocket and he pulled out a bottle.

He handed them to Jay. "Take these to Dr. Sanders. I got them in Memphis," John said. He paused. "A doctor heard about Sarah Jane. I think this is new medicine. Dr. Sanders should look at it before you give it to Sarah Jane."

Jay took the matchboxes and the bottle. "What is it?" he asked.

John turned away from Jay and he began to take his coat off. "I don't know. Dr. Sanders will know what to do. The pills need to be crushed and mixed with the whiskey," he said. "There are instructions in one of the matchboxes."

John placed his coat on his chair. He took off his hat and sat at his desk. "I hope it helps," John added.

Jay nodded his head. He started to walk to the door when he stopped and turned. "Come before sun set! She don't show until sun set. She just stands and waits," Jay said.

"I'll be there!" John answered.

Jay nodded and he walked out the door. When Jay had closed the door, John quickly stood. He walked to the door and he locked it. He pulled the shade down. John walked to his bedroom and he pulled a large box from under his bed. He took the box to his desk and he opened it. The box was filled with twelve gauge shotgun shells.

He reached for his coat pocket and he removed the bag of dimes. He stacked the dimes on his desk in rows of five each. Then, he opened one of the shells. He poured the shot in his coffee cup and he replaced the shot with five dimes. He closed the shell and he opened another.

It took John about one hour to prepare the shells. He opened one of his desk drawers and he removed two leather cartridge holders. The cartridge holders were filled with shells. He removed the shells and he replaced them with the ones he had prepared. There were several dimes left and he opened several of the older shells and he replaced the dimes. He replaced all of the shells in the holders. When he had finished, he took his gun and he began to clean it.

Night of the Double Moon

I kept getting more ill. The days passed and the double moon was coming. It was before the double moon that she came. The sun would set and she would appear near the woods. The woods weren't far from our front gate. She would stand near the woods and watch the house. When the sun set, Andy would appear. He stood near the gate. Andy would walk back and forth in front of the gate.

When the sun rose, Andy would crow. It was a loud crow. It was like a victory call. When Andy crowed, she would disappear. People began talking about the ghost woman. I remember several people coming to our house to see her. They would wait for the sun to set and then they would see her. She would be near the edge of the woods. She would stand and look toward our house.

When the people saw her, they would leave. They did not come back.

The story spread that I was dying and the ghost woman was waiting for me to die. Someone said she was waiting for the night of the double moon. The double moon had something to do with witches and ghosts. It was the night of the double moon that spirits were held in limbo. The spirit just sat and waited for someone or something to collect it.

She was going to get mine.

People stopped coming to our house to see me. Everyone stopped coming except John Stepp. He came every day. I remember him leaning over my bed. He would say something to me but I don't know what he said. I was real ill. I would get real hot then I would get real cold. He came for several days, then he stopped coming. He did not visit for several days.

John Stepp never visited at night. He never came to see the ghost woman. My mother said he was afraid of her. My father said John Stepp was busy watching the young boys. He would drive his car near the woods to make sure the young boys weren't out after dark. My father said John Stepp was up all night. He slept during the day.

My father said John Stepp didn't believe in ghosts or the ghost woman. He thought it was some light or something we were seeing. If we believed she was coming to get me the night of the double moon, he would come and watch over me. He didn't believe in ghosts but he would come to make us feel better.

Andy quit coming to my window. He would come at sunset and stay by the gate. Andy would walk back and forth in front of the gate. I remember asking for Andy. My brother J.B. said Andy was busy. He was busy keeping the ghost woman from getting me.

I would wake up in the morning when I heard Andy crow. When Andy crowed, the first light came through my window. His crow was real loud. It was a victory call.

The night of the double moon was that night. I remember hearing my mother and father arguing. John Stepp was coming that night. He was going to watch over me. My mother didn't want him to come. I remember my mother yelling at my father. "John Stepp ain't worth a damn! He never did anything for anybody," she yelled. My father didn't yell back. He was afraid of John Stepp.

It was the night of the double moon when John came to our house. I was real ill. I remember my mother yelling at my father that she didn't want John Stepp in our house. She was afraid he would steal something. I remember John knocking on our door. The sun had almost set. My mother went to the door. I heard her speak in a real sweet voice. "Hello John! Come in! I made you some coffee!" she said.

I could hear the heavy steps of John Stepp on our wooden floor. Dr. Sanders had visited earlier. He had some medicine with him and he made me take it. It tasted real bad. I got sick at my stomach and I threw most of it up. Dr. Sanders gave me more. He waited a while then he left.

My head felt real light and I felt dizzy. I remember seeing John Stepp leaning toward me. He said something but I don't remember what he said. I saw him sit in a chair near the door. I remember being afraid. I was afraid of John Stepp. He sat in that chair with his gun in his hands. Then, I feel asleep.

The sun had set when J.B. ran to John Stepp. "She's here!" he said. "She's standing by the woods!"

John stood. He walked to the door and he looked toward the woods. He could see a white figure near the edge. He looked close. It was a woman! She was wearing a long, white dress. She was standing at the edge of the woods and she was looking toward the house.

John saw something else. He saw a white rooster at the gate. The rooster was walking back and forth in front of the gate. The rooster looked like he was guarding the gate.

He walked out the door and he walked to the gate. He could see the woman better. She was young, maybe nineteen. She had long, black hair and she looked pretty. John looked at the rooster. The rooster walked back and forth in front of the gate.

"Wait here!" John said to the rooster.

The woman stood near the edge of the woods. As John approached she looked at him. She had a smile on her face. John got closer then, she began to move away. John watched her move. Her dress was long and it touched the ground. She did not appear to walk backward. She just moved backward.

John reached into his coat pocket and he removed his badge. He held it toward the woman. "My name is John Stepp. I am the constable," he said. "Who are you?"

The woman didn't answer. John could see her face. She was very pretty. He had never seen her before.

John started to walk toward her and she moved backward. He stopped. When he stopped, she stopped. John started walking backward. As he moved backward, she moved forward. John watched her move forward. The dress she wore was white. It was long and it touched the ground. He looked to see her knees. If she walked forward, he should see her knees move under the dress. He saw no knees. She just moved forward.

John moved backward. She moved to the edge of the woods and she stopped. John stopped. "Who are you?" John commanded.

The woman did not answer. She stood at the edge of the woods. There was a smile on her face. She smiled at John Stepp.

John chuckled. "That proves it!" he said. "She's a ghost! No woman living ever smiled at me like that."

He reached into his right coat pocket. In his right coat pocket were several dimes. He took one and he flipped it toward her. She didn't move. John took another dime and he flipped it toward her. She didn't move.

John reached into his left coat pocket. In his coat pocket were two dimes. He took one and he flipped it toward her. It was dark and John couldn't see where the dime went. He looked at the woman. She looked upward as if she could see it. Then, she moved sideways. She moved sideways away from the dime he had flipped at her.

When she moved sideways, she just moved. She didn't turn or look to the side. She just moved. John looked at her dress. He looked to see her legs move. He saw no movement where her knees should be. The dress just moved. She just moved sideways.

John chuckled. He reached into his right coat pocket and he flipped another dime at her. She did not move. He flipped another one, she did not move. He reached into his left coat pocket. He had one dime left. He flipped it at her.

When he flipped the dime at her, she looked upward as if she could see it. Then she moved backward and to the side. He looked at her face.

There was a snarl on her face! She had a look of hatred and fear on her face.

"That's more like it!" John chuckled. "That's the way women look at me."

John reached into his right coat pocket and he pulled the dimes out. He looked at them. They were the dimes he removed from his shotgun shells. The two dimes in his left pocket were two he had left over. The two dimes in his left pocket were two of the dimes Father Oliver blessed. The two dimes had been sprinkled with Holy water and blessed.

He started to walk toward her and she moved backward. John kept walking and she kept moving backward. He walked to the edge of the woods. She moved backward into the woods and she went behind several large trees.

John followed her. He walked to where he had last seen her. She was gone! He couldn't see her anywhere. He walked around the woods looking for her. He didn't see her. She was gone!

John walked back to the gate where J.B. was waiting for him. When John reached the gate, J.B. pointed toward the woods. "She's back!" he said.

John turned to look at the woods. She was standing where he had first seen her. He looked at J.B. and the rooster. "I make you official deputies!" he said. John kneeled downward to the rooster.

"Deputy Rooster! Your job is to let us know if she starts to come toward the house!" he said.

"Andy!" J.B. said. "His name is Andy! Sarah Jane named him Andy."

"Sorry," John said. "Deputy Andy, your job is to let us know if she starts to come toward the house."

John stood and he picked up a large rock near the gate. He walked toward the woman. He came real close and she began to move away. John placed the rock on the ground. "I don't know who are or what you are. It doesn't matter! If you pass this rock, I'll kill you!" John said.

John walked to his car. He opened the trunk and he removed a large bag. He returned to the gate and he knelled beside Andy. John pointed toward the rock.

"Deputy Andy, if she starts to move toward the house let us know. If she passes that rock, make as much noise as you can," he said.

"What are you going to do?" J.B. asked.

"I warned her not to pass that rock," John said.

"What happens if she passes that rock?" J.B. asked.

"I'll kill her!" John Stepp replied.

"She's already dead! How can you kill a ghost?" J.B. asked.

"I don't think she's a ghost. If she is a real ghost, why is she afraid of me? Why is she afraid of Andy?" John asked J.B.

"Everybody's afraid of you!" J.B. said.

John Stepp laughed. "There are many types of fear. Right now your mother and father are afraid your sister is going to die. There is no shame in that kind of fear. That woman is something else. I figure she is afraid of me and Andy because we ain't afraid of her," he said.

John Stepp was holding his gun. J.B. pointed at his gun. "She's afraid of your gun that shoots dimes," he said.

John Stepp stood. "She had better be afraid of it!" he snarled. "If she passes that rock, I'll blow her back to the hell she came from!"

John and J.B. walked into the house. "Deputy J.B., I need you to stand by the door and watch her. If Deputy Andy starts making noise, let me know," John ordered.

J.B. stood by the opened door. He looked toward the ghost woman.

John opened the bag. Inside were two leather shell holders. He placed one across his shoulder and he placed one near the door of my bedroom.

He came and sat in my bedroom. He sat near the door and held his gun in his hands.

My brother J. B. stood at the door watching her. It was close to dawn when I became very ill. My mother and father thought I was going to die. My fever was real high and they washed me with cold, wet rags. They gave me some of the medicine Dr. Sanders brought me. My two sisters were standing near my bed. They cried.

It was before dawn when Andy started making a lot of noise. J.B. had fallen asleep. He was sitting in a chair near the door when he fell asleep. The noise Andy made woke him. She began to come toward the house. My brother yelled for John Stepp.

John quickly left my bedside. He took the second belt of shells and put it over his shoulder and he cocked his gun. He cocked both barrels. John quickly ran toward the door and he ran to the gate. He and Andy stood by the gate.

The woman was moving toward the gate. John could see her face. She was not smiling, she was snarling! He watched her move. Closer and closer she came to the rock he had placed in the road. When she passed the rock, he fired his gun.

Kaboom! Kaboom!

John held his gun against his hip. He felt the gun jerk as the two shells were fired. He had aimed it high. It was aimed too high to strike her. If she was a crazy woman, he didn't want to hurt her. He only wanted to frighten her.

The dimes made a whistling sound. They went high into the air then they struck the tall trees. There was a noise of cracking tree limbs. The dimes smashed into the trees. John had placed additional powder in the shells. There was smoke.

The woman kept coming! John opened the breech of his gun and the two shells ejected. He quickly replaced them and he fired again.

Kaboom! Kaboom!

The gun was aimed high. The dimes smashed into the tops of the trees. He quickly ejected the two shells and reloaded. She kept coming!

John began to walk forward. As he walked forward, he fired and reloaded. Each shot was aimed high. The dimes smashed into the tops of the trees. If she was a crazy woman he only wanted to frighten her. He did not want to kill her.

Closer and closer John came to her. He could see her face. She had a snarl on her face. She was not afraid of him! Her arms were outstretched in front of her. She held her hands as to grab him. She kept coming! John loaded and fired. Each shot was aimed high. The dimes smashed into the tops of the trees. The smoke from the shots was thick.

They met in the middle. There was less than twenty feet between them. John looked at her. She had a snarl on her face and her hands were outstretched in front of her. He looked at her dress. There was no movement where her legs should be. She just moved forward.

As she neared, John raised his gun toward her. He aimed his gun at her face. She was less than ten feet from him. He stopped and waited for her to come to him.

"I warned you!" John yelled. She was real close to him and John cocked both barrels. Then, something white jumped in front of him.

It was Andy!

The woman did not notice Andy. As John walked toward the woman Andy walked right beside him. The woman didn't notice Andy walking beside John. She was looking at John Stepp. She was watching his gun. As John walked forward, he fired both barrels. He quickly reloaded and fired again. Andy walked beside John.

She had a snarl on her face and her hands were outstretched to grab him. She reached toward John when Andy jumped at her.

Andy jumped high into the air. Her arms were held outward and Andy jumped between her arms. He spurred her! Andy tore into her chest with his razor sharp spurs. He tore into her throat and her chest.

John saw Andy's wings flapping. He couldn't see the woman's face from Andy's wings. Andy was spurring her! John could hear the sound of something being ripped. Her arms were held outward and Andy was between her arms. Andy tore into her throat and her chest with his razor sharp spurs. Then, Andy plunged his two right spurs deep into her chest. He stabbed her in the heart!

"Ahhhhhhhhhh!" a horrible, terrible scream could be heard.

John's gun fired.

Kaboom! Kaboom!

John held his gun with his right hand. His gun was aimed at her face and it was held at arm's length. When the shots were fired, the gun kicked backward. The gun smoke blew backward into John's face. He felt the acrid powders strike his face and he jerked his head backward.

John turned his head forward. His eyes were burning and he couldn't see. He crouched on the ground and quickly ejected the two shells and reloaded. She was near! He knew it! John crouched on the ground and he held his gun upward as he cocked both barrels.

John's eyes began to clear. There was nothing!

The smoke was clearing. There was nothing there! He quickly turned toward the house. He didn't see her! He could see J.B. standing in the doorway. The door was partially closed. She couldn't have passed him.

He quickly stood and he turned in all directions. He saw nothing.

Then, he heard it! It was a rooster's crow. It was loud, very loud. John looked in all directions. The sound seemed to come from everywhere. He looked for Andy. He wasn't there!

John looked toward the horizon as the sun broke through the trees. The first rays of sun shined through the trees. The sun struck his eyes and he blinked.

John stood for a minute. He looked all around. They were gone! Andy and the woman were gone!

John walked toward the house. When he came to the door, J.B. was standing and watching. "What was that scream?" J.B. asked.

John turned toward the woods. "It was an owl. One of those dimes must have struck an owl," John said.

J.B. looked toward the woods. "Didn't sound like no owl to me!" he said.

J.B. opened the door. "Who was it?" he asked.

John looked at J.B. "Nothing," he said. "It was some kind of light. There was no ghost woman. It was nothing."

John looked toward the woods. "I'm sorry about Andy!" he said. "He got in front of me. I hit him! I think I saw him head for the woods."

J.B. looked at John and he shrugged his shoulders. "We never see him after the sun comes up. That was Andy crowing. We will see him when the sun sets," J.B. said.

John looked at J.B. "I don't think so. I don't think he'll be back," John said.

My father came running toward the door. He had a big smile on his face. "Her fever broke! The medicine Dr. Sanders brought seemed to have helped. I think she's going to be OK," my father said.

John looked at my father. "It was nothing but some kind of light. I think I hit Andy with one of my shots. I thought I saw him head for the woods," John said.

John Stepp turned. He walked to his car and he cranked it. Then, he drove away.

John drove to the Hibdon Cemetery. He walked to the graves of Randall, George, and Abram. He looked at their graves. They were undisturbed. He walked to where he had found the three boys. He looked around. John didn't know what he was looking for. He just looked. Then, he drove to one of the farmers that raised chickens.

It was noon before John returned to see me. The medicine really helped. I felt better. J.B. said he drove up to the house and he opened his car trunk. In his trunk was a dead rooster. The rooster had been shot to pieces. There wasn't much left. J.B. and my father came to his car.

John pointed at the dead rooster. "I'm sorry about Andy. He must have gotten in front of me when I fired that last shot," John said. "I found him in the woods."

J.B. looked at the dead rooster.

"That's OK," my father said. "He was just a pet and he came and went. Sarah Jane knew one day he would not come. Just bury him."

J.B. looked at the dead rooster. "That's not Andy!" he said.

John looked at J.B. "It's Andy! I found him in the woods," he said.

J.B. pointed toward the dead rooster's leg. "Andy had two spurs on each leg. This rooster only has one. It's not Andy!" J.B. said.

John closed the trunk. "I'll bury him," he said.

John Stepp never came into our house. J. B. said he asked about me. J.B. said he stood a long time looking at the woods near our gate. He looked at the woods, and then he just drove away. I never saw him again. I never saw him, after that night. My last memory of seeing John Stepp was John sitting in that chair in my room. In his hands, he held his gun that shot dimes.

It was many days before I was well enough to sit up. I heard the bad news about John Stepp. He died in a car accident. He died several days after that night. My father said he was driving real fast when he lost control of his car. People thought he was chasing some moonshiners. No one really knew.

No one went to John Stepp's funeral. My mother and father didn't go. I don't think anybody went except Brandon. Brandon closed the Texaco filling station and he went to the funeral. I know this because my father was angry with Brandon. My father was to deliver feed that day. He stopped for gasoline and the station was closed. My father couldn't deliver feed because he needed gasoline for the truck.

John Stepp was buried in his family's cemetery. They lived neared Jefferson. Several weeks after

John was buried a priest came to his grave. The priest said a lot of strange words and waved a smoking ball over the grave. Then, he sprinkled water on the grave. No one knew who the priest was. The priest didn't say anything to anyone. He came to the grave and did strange things over it. No one was Catholic and we didn't know what he did. I would learn years later that the priest blessed the grave.

Weeks passed and I got better. I returned to school. The sheriff sent someone to Gladeville to replace John Stepp. I don't remember who he was. One day he visited me. He seemed nice. He was not as tall as John Stepp was and he didn't have a gun that shot dimes. I don't remember him.

The Election

The elections were coming and there were several men running for constable. I was feeling well and my family and I went to town to hear speeches.

There were many people there to listen. The men made promises. One man was talking and no one was listening. They didn't listen until the man mentioned John Stepp.

"This town needs law and order!" the man yelled. "You need someone strong and brave! You don't need another John Stepp!"

"What about John Stepp?" one of the men in the crowd yelled.

The man laughed. "I know John Stepp! I backed him down!" he yelled.

"When?" one of the men in the crowd yelled.

"I was a constable in Jackson," he yelled. "John Stepp should have been in Gladeville protecting you folks! There were three murders in Gladeville and John Stepp was in Jackson. He was asleep and drunk in his car. He was too drunk to drive and he stopped his car near Jackson."

"Liar!" one of the men in the crowd yelled. "I never saw John Stepp take a drink!"

"Let him speak!" another man in the crowd yelled.

The man laughed. "I ordered John Stepp out of his car. I ordered him to raise his hands," he yelled.

"What happened?" one of the men yelled.

"He raised his hands. He was afraid of me," the man yelled.

Miss. Louise was in the crowd listening to the speeches. "Liar!" Miss. Louise yelled. "You're a liar! John Stepp wouldn't raise his hands to any man."

The man began to get nervous. "It's true," he yelled. "He raised his hands. I let him go when I saw his badge. It was a professional courtesy."

"Liar!" many people in the crowd yelled.

"Boo!" many of the people in the crowd yelled.

Mr. Benson was in the crowd. He yelled at the people, "I didn't like John Stepp but this man is a liar! John Stepp wouldn't raise his hands for any man. I never saw him take a drink. This man is a liar!"

"It's true!" the man yelled. "I was a constable! I have a witness!"

The people booed the man. He ran quickly from the stage.

When the ballots were cast, the man got no votes not even his own. He didn't mark his name. The people of Gladeville didn't like John Stepp but no one was going to say he was a coward and a drunk. Not even after he was dead.

Faded Memories

My father died at the age of eighty-four. He died in the Veterans Hospital in Murfreesboro. My father was in World War I. I was nine months old when he returned from the war.

My father didn't talk much about the war. When he did, he would talk about one battle. In the battle, he and the other farm boys drove the mules that pulled the big guns. There was a battle near a forest in Germany. The German soldiers shot the mules that pulled one of the big guns. They also shot several of the farm boys driving the mules.

The men were ordered to move the gun toward the woods. They cut the harness of the dead mules and they pulled the mules and the dead soldiers to the side. Then, they began to push the big gun up a hill toward the woods.

The German soldiers were shooting at them as they pushed the big gun up the hill. Many of the men were killed. My father said the men were crying as they pushed the big gun. They could not stop to help the wounded. They had to get the big gun into position to fire into the woods.

My father was shot pushing that big gun. He was shot in the knee. They never removed the bullet. My father carried that bullet the rest of his life.

When my father told the story he would cry. Many of his friends were killed pushing that big gun. His best friend Jacob was killed. Jacob was shot and he lay to the side yelling for help. The soldiers couldn't stop to help. My father couldn't stop to help. They had to push that big gun up the hill. When my father was shot, he fell to the side. When he crawled to Jacob, Jacob was dead.

Those farm boys got that big gun up the hill. When it was in position, they fired the big gun at the German soldiers. The shells of that big gun tore a hole in the German defense. The shells of that big gun pushed the German soldiers back.

My father would tell the story and cry.

I saw my father cry one other time. He cried when Dr. Sanders died. We all went to the funeral. My father cried because Dr. Sanders saved me that night. He brought me medicine that cured me. My father never talked about John Stepp, or that night, he talked about Dr. Sanders. He talked about Dr. Sanders bringing me that medicine.

My father said Dr. Sanders charged him ten dollars for that medicine and it was the best ten dollars he ever spent. He also said the whiskey was the best he ever drank. The pills were crushed and mixed with whiskey. When the medicine was gone, there were two swallows of whiskey left. My father drank it! He said it was real smooth!

My mother lived to be ninety-two. She died in a nursing home. When she was younger, she lived with my family and me. She was still able to talk and think. I remember asking her about that night. She said it never happened. I asked about those three boys that died. She remembered that. I asked her about that rooster I had as a pet. She remembered that. I asked her about John Stepp coming to our home. She got real angry and she crossed her arms. "John Stepp wasn't worth a damn!" she said. "He never did anything for anybody. He never came to our house! I wouldn't let him in the door."

My brother J.B died when he was eighty-two. He died of lung cancer. J.B. smoked all his life. He started when he was ten. When he was still well, I visited him several times. He had a small garden and we picked corn and tomatoes. We were sitting at the eating table when we started talking about that night. J.B. said it never happened. I asked him about John Stepp coming to our house. J.B. said, "There are some things left well enough alone."

I visited my younger sister before J.B. died and I asked her about that night. She didn't remember much. I asked her if anybody came to our house. She said, "Yes!" I asked her if she remembered who it was. She thought it was the sheriff.

I asked her if she remembered John Stepp. My sister grunted, "John Stepp wasn't worth a damn! He never did anything for anybody."

She started laughing. "You must be talking about that witch woman that tried to take you," she said. "You need to talk to J.B.! J.B. can tell you all about it. I think he still has one."

"One what?" I asked.

"One of those dimes John Stepp fired at the witch woman!" she said. "J.B. dug one of them out of a tree, in the woods, near our gate."

"He kept the dime in that bottle near his pictures until it fell and broke. He was offered five hundred dollars for that bottle," she added.

What bottle?" I asked.

"The bottle Dr. Sanders brought with him that night," she said. "It was full of whiskey. The whiskey came from over seas and it was real old. The man, who tired to buy the bottle, told J.B. if the whiskey was still in it, he would give him five thousand dollars for it. It was old! Real old!"

J.B. died before I could ask him about that dime and that old bottle.

Sometimes I dream about that night. I wake up in a cold sweat. I wake up with my body drenched in sweat and I am afraid. My body jerks upward as I remember that night. I remember the sound of John Stepp's gun and I remember that horrible scream.

I remember the sound of Andy's crow and the light of morning shining through my window. Andy's crow was louder than I had ever heard it. It was a victory call! When I heard Andy's crow, I wasn't afraid anymore. Somehow, I felt safe.

Nobody ever said anything good about John Stepp. People said he wasn't worth a damn. People said he never did anything for anybody. He did something for me! When I was nine years old, he fought the ghost woman for my soul.

The Author

Sarah Jane Singer

Sarah Jane Singer was born in the year 1919. As a young girl, she lived in the areas of Smyrna, LaVergne, Gladeville, Mount Juliet, and Norene, Tennessee. She currently lives in the small town of Lebanon, Tennessee.

Sarah Jane was very ill as a young girl. She was ill with pneumonia nine times before she was twenty. Sarah Jane never completed the fourth grade.

It wasn't until she was eighty-four years old that she began to write. Sarah Jane writes about stories that she has heard and events she has personal knowledge of. When she was nine years old, she became very ill.

As she lay near death, Sarah Jane claims a ghost woman came to take her spirit. She claims the ghost woman came to the woods near the gate to their house and stood waiting. The ghost woman waited for Sarah

Jane to die. The ghost woman came to take her spirit the night of the double moon.

Night of the Double Moon - A Real Ghost Story is gleaned from events she has personal knowledge of and stories she had heard of the people involved. Most notably, Constable John Stepp, the person no one liked.

Sarah Jane's story is one of horror and unexplained events. It is a story that does not lend itself to imagination.

Published Books

Two Bullets for Sergeant Franks

In 1864, a drought in the area of Gladeville, Tennessee caused a small lake to recede. What lay at the bottom of the lake shook the foundations of the community. What lay at the bottom of the lake brought hundreds of Union soldiers to the small community of Gladeville.

The bottom of the small lake held more than one hundred Union soldiers. The soldiers were placed in cloth bags. They died by being struck in the back of their heads by a blunt tool - a shovel.

Union soldiers gathered the people together to determine who did this thing. There were no young men in Gladeville; the men were at war. Only old men, women, and children remained.

Union soldiers gathered the people into the Gladeville Church. They were questioned. They were threatened. No one knew anything about what lay on the bottom of the small lake.

The Union soldiers determined that scavengers did this thing. What lay on the bottom of the lake was kept a secret. A secret so horrible no one spoke of it.

Among the old men, women and children, gathered in the Gladeville Church, were two young women Victoria and Candis. What the people of Gladeville never discovered, and what the Union soldiers did not know, is that Victoria and Candis did this thing.